I0553232

My Love, My Heart

Copyright

Disclaimer

The books in this series are based completely on dreams that I've had or that one of the other people in my relationship has had. They all have a little bit of real life thrown in so that you, the reader, can get to know us a little bit better.

These books can and should be read as standalone books. There isn't an order to them. All of the characters in the books are the same, as they are all based on characters from real life.

As you read these books, please keep in mind that other than the characters and the city they are based in, these books are not connected to other books in the series. They aren't a continuation of other books. They are all novellas based on dreams that revolve around the same characters.

As you keep that in mind, please enjoy reading this book. I do hope you will also read the others in this series and love them as much as I loved writing them!

Opening Quote

It's strange. I feel like I've known you before. And I want to understand you. More and more. When I'm with you, I feel like a magical child. Everything strange. Everything wild. Rain is what the thunder brings. For the first time I can hear my heart sing. Call me a fool, but I know I'm not.

Rain by Madonna

Chapter One

☆ Mariah ☆

"I'm so excited to try the Lo Mein and Egg Foo Yung. Oh! And the Cream Cheese Wontons!" my girlfriend says to me as she bounces, excitedly on her heels. I love when she gets excited like that. Mixed with her adorable British accent, and her easily excitable persona, Lyric Sharpe is my dream. My fantasy.

I laugh at myself because I never in a million years thought for a second this would be me. I was married... to a guy. Now, here I am in a relationship with a beautiful woman. I couldn't be happier, but it's not where I thought I would end up. I honestly believed I would be miserable the rest of my life married to a man who didn't treat me with the respect I deserve.

I shake my head as I kiss Lyric. I run my hands through her dark brown hair as I deepen the kiss. She pulls away, and I moan. "Why is it always so hard to stop kissing you? Even after a year of being together?"

She blushes. It only succeeds in making me want her even more. "You always flatter me."

I smile as I kiss her softly again. "I'll be back. I wish this place delivered. It's always so busy, and I hate people."

5

"I would go, but…" She chews on her lip and casts her gorgeous golden hazel eyes to the ground.

"I know. I haven't had time to bring you out to learn. But with this last book coming out and a break between for our cruise, I'll have plenty of time. Especially with plotting this new series." I smile. Her eyes light up, and I melt slightly at that pretty sparkle that always shines when she's happy.

"I'm so proud of you. You're doing so well with your two series out."

"I'm doing better than I imagined, but I couldn't without you keeping me on track."

"You do all the hard work, baby. I'm just here to make you look good."

"Well, you make me look very good." My cheeks redden a little, and I take a deep breath. "Ugh. Off I go."

"Are you sure you don't want me to come with you?"

I shake my head. "No. We need someone here when maintenance shows up to fix the air conditioner."

"Right. I forgot we needed to be here."

"It's okay. I won't be long. Matt is across the hall if maintenance gets here before me. If they make you nervous, you can grab him."

Matt.

Lieutenant Matt Chance of the Gainesville Police Department. Lyric and I both have quite the crush on him. We talk about him all the time. I don't know if Matt has any idea, but Lyric and I may or may not fantasize a lot about him. Sometimes, when we're messing around with our vibrators, we pretend it's him. Crazy? Probably. But it satisfies the craving we have for our sexy neighbor.

I steel myself for the crowd I know I'm going to face at China 88 as Lyric smiles and nods. That place is always so, so busy. At least I have the drive to psych myself up.

"Hurry back!" Lyric slaps my ass on my way out the door.

I squeak and laugh. "Lyric!"

She bites her lip and shrugs with wide, innocent eyes. "What?"

"You're so bad," I tease as I grab my keys.

"You love it."

6

"Incredibly." I close the door behind me with a last soft smile over my shoulder as she giggles and curls up on our couch in her sexy gray bootie shorts and tight as sin purple tank top. I enter the elevator thinking of her perfectly large, round tits, and how they fill out her tank top. She rarely ever wears a bra. She hates them.

I bite my lip and smile to myself as the elevator stops on the ground floor of our apartment building. I don't know how I got so lucky. Lyric is worlds above me when it comes to looks. Who am I kidding? She's worlds above me on pretty much everything. I must have done something right in my past life to deserve a woman like her.

I close the car door and pull out of my parking space. I was trained when I started driving to never pull into a place I will have to back out of. Most accidents occur when the driver is backing up. Of course learning how to drive from a police officer probably has a little to do with that.

I pull onto 13th Street and sigh. The only thing I miss about my old life is the few friends and few family members who were actually around for me when I needed someone. Everyone else can go to hell for all I care. They don't deserve me. It took me a long time to realize that, but with Lyric's help, I'm starting to understand that everything I went through wasn't and isn't my fault.

Moving to Gainesville, Florida, was the second best decision I ever made. The first was for sure admitting my feelings for Lyric. I've never known a love like what she's shown me. I didn't know a love like her existed. I still don't think I'm worthy of her.

As I anticipated, China 88 is busy. As usual. It doesn't take me long to get my food since I ordered ahead, but there's so many people. I'm cursed with anxiety disorder and large crowds are a trigger.

"Stupid people," I mutter under my breath as I get elbowed in the chest on my way out the door. I nearly drop my bag of food and bite my cheek to stop myself from crying. I don't get takeout for a reason. It involves leaving the comfort of my home and the safety of my love's arms to go out and battle society when they're hungry. Everyone is grumpier when they're hungry.

Lyric texts me, and I smile.

Lyric: Are you doing okay, love?

I get back into the car and breathe deeply for a few moments. She knows. She always knows when I need her.

7

Mariah: I'm okay, babe. There's a lot of people. I'm on my way home.

I put my phone on the seat next to me and pull out of the parking lot. The further away I get from the restaurant, the better I feel. My hands unclench around the wheel the more I relax. I start breathing more normally.

Ahead of me, I see blue and red flashing lights, so I immediately slow down. I start to pull over into the other lane when something odd catches my eye.

"Is that…?" I squint as I slow further. "Oh my God!"

Adrenaline, training, and instinct immediately take over, and suddenly I'm not in control of my actions anymore. I pull over behind the squad car and jump out. The officer is in a fight seemingly for his life. He's on his knees in the ditch with some guy standing over him. The cop is swinging and keeping a grip on the guy. His fists are connecting, and he's trying to get up.

I run towards the officer as the guy kicks him over and over in the chest and face. The officer doesn't let go of the guy, and despite how many blows he's taking, he's still trying to get to his feet. I glance over my shoulder at all of the cars driving by. How is no one stopping? How can anyone see this and not want to help? Am I crazy for interjecting myself in a fight with two guys who are at least a foot taller than I am and definitely far more muscular?

The officer gets to his feet, but I can tell he's weakened and getting tired. The guy goes for his gun. The officer punches him, but the guy manages to get a hold of it anyway. The closer I get to them, the more my own training kicks in. I went to school to be a cop at one point in my life. This. Right here. This is the reason I never became one.

"Let go! Let the gun go!" the officer grunts.

"Fuck you!" The guy yanks the gun away as he knees the officer as hard as I think he possibly could in the stomach. The officer loses his grip on the gun with the combination of the guy twisting the gun and the force of the knee strike.

"Fuck! No!" the officer yells as he immediately lunges for the gun. The guy turns the gun on the officer just as I reach them both. What took seconds feels like it took minutes to me, but I know I need to help.

The officer gets hold of the gun once more, but the guy punches him hard in the face. He staggers back and sinks to his knees. I don't think. I only act. I duck low and spear the guy. I connect with his stomach with as much force as I can muster as I grab the gun. It goes off. I scream, praying to whatever God is listening that the bullet didn't hit the officer.

"What the fuck?" the guy groans as we both hit the ground. I have the gun in my hand. I twist and yank it away with all of my strength as I scramble to my feet. Out of the corner of my eye, I see the officer collapse on the ground. Blood is covering his eye and the side of his head. I level the gun on the guy as I walk backwards to the officer.

"Don't move!" I yell at him. He sees the gun and, thankfully, chooses to stay still. I kneel next to the officer, keeping one eye on the guy, and check on him. "Thank God," I whisper when I feel a pulse.

"Thank you," he whimpers. "Thank fucking God for you." I can barely hear him as I sink further down next to him. I gently touch his head looking at how deep the gash on it is.

"You're bleeding really bad," I say quietly. He reaches weakly for his radio and misses several times. "Let me." I gingerly take his radio from his shoulder, keeping the gun trained on the guy. "Officer down. Officer down," I say into the radio. "Corner of Northeast 3rd Street and Northeast 2nd Avenue. Officer has a head injury, but is conscious. One suspect being held at gunpoint by a citizen using the officer's gun. Send back-up and EMTs."

The radio crackles to life. "All units. Officer down at the corner of Northeast 3rd Street and Northeast 2nd Avenue. All units. Officer down at the corner of Northeast 3rd Street and Northeast 2nd Avenue. Suspect being held at gunpoint by a citizen"

I put the radio back on the officer's shoulder and force myself to take deep breaths. The adrenaline is starting to wear off, and all I can think about is the rising panic that's taking its place. I shake my head slightly and focus. The guy. I need to keep the guy away from the officer. Away from us. Why is he smiling? Is he a maniac? Does he know something I don't?

Training. Focus on my training. "Stay where you are! Keep your hands where I can see them!" I yell with as much authority as I can manage when I see him shift. My hand shakes. My hand never shakes.

Lyric.

9

I won't let myself get hurt. I won't leave her. I need to protect myself and this officer so I can go home. Why is he smiling?

I hear sirens in the distance. Thank God. Oh, thank you. Tears sting my eyes. I glance down at the officer as he groans. "Still with me?" I ask, choking back a sob.

"I'm dizzy as fuck. Can't see straight." The officer coughs and groans.

"Please, please hang in there."

"Keep the gun on him," he whispers.

"You planning on shooting me in the back if I run, crazy bitch?"

"I plan on shooting if you so much as move," I growl with narrowed eyes. I need to focus on protecting us.

"I bet you couldn't hit me."

"Please. Try me. I've had more training with shooting a gun than I bet this officer here has."

The guy laughs and begins to stand. He'd been kneeling so nicely on his knees. "You won't shoot."

I shoot the ground next to his foot; he yelps. The officer jumps. They guy sinks to his knees and raises his hands above his head glaring at me, but slightly fearful.

"Next time I'll aim for your dick." I may be scared to death. I may be fighting off a major panic attack. But I'm going home. This guy isn't getting away, and this officer will go home to his family if it's the last thing I do. "I assure you, I'm quite proficient with a gun."

The guy has the decency to not say a word or move. The sirens get closer and closer. The minutes turn into seconds until, finally, I hear screeching brakes. Several squad cars converge on the area.

"Miss? Give me the gun, please," a deep male voice says next to me. I look up at the older officer with kind eyes and let him take the gun. He gives me a hand up as other officers arrest the guy and EMTs tend to the injured officer. I watch, feeling a sense of responsibility for him, as they load him onto a stretcher.

"Wait," he says, looking at me. He reaches out a hand. I take it and smile softly. "Thank you. I don't know who you are, but thank fucking God you stopped."

I reach down and brush his short, dark brown hair from his forehead. "Anytime."

"Who are you? What's your name?"

"Mariah."

"Mariah. I'm DJ. Thank you."

"We need to go. He needs to get checked out," one of the EMTs says.

I nod as I let go of his hand. "I'm glad you're okay, DJ."

"I'm glad you stopped, Mariah."

The EMTs rush him away, and I swallow down more panic trying to rise to the surface. I've gotten really good at fighting them off. There was a period of time I couldn't, but Lyric helped. She's always given me strength.

It seems like hours before the police finally let me go from the scene. I've only been able to text Lyric to tell her I'd been tied up and would be awhile. I told her I'd explain later, but I know her. She's worried sick by now. I climb in my car and call her as I pull away from the scene.

"Mariah? Oh my God! What happened? It's been over an hour!" Lyric's panicked voice fills my car.

I bite my lip. "I saw an officer in trouble. I stopped to help. He was really hurt. He was fighting so hard. The guy went for his gun and everything. I couldn't just drive by."

"Are you okay? Are you hurt? How's the officer? Did they get the guy? Mariah, I'm so worried!"

"I'm a little teary, but I'm okay. They took the officer to the hospital, and the guy was arrested. I'll explain everything when I get home. I'm so sorry it's been so long."

"I'm glad you're okay, honey."

"Me, too. I love you."

"I love you, too."

I hang up and glance in my rear-view mirror. I've been keeping an eye on this black SUV following me ever since I left the scene. He's made every turn I have even though I've made very random turns. I'm convinced I'm being followed.

My heart races out of control as the realization hits me. I can't stop it this time. It feels like it's going to pound out of my chest. I hit the gas and speed through the streets for home.

"Oh God. No. No. They aren't following me. They can't be."

But they are. I know it deep down. They are. Should I call the police? Should I call Lyric? Should I keep driving, and hope I lose them?

I shake my head and focus. Almost there. Almost home. I speed into the parking lot of Arbor Park Apartments and slam on my brakes as I whip between two cars. I jump out of my car, forgetting completely about the food on the passenger seat. I duck down low and watch as the black SUV squeals its tires and speeds down the street.

I gasp for breath as I watch them until they disappear into the distance. My head spins, and my throat closes up. My vision gets blurry.

Lyric.

I have to get to Lyric.

I whimper as I pull myself into the elevator. I shake my head several times and refuse to close my eyes.

Breathe. I need to breathe. I need to… breathe. I need to focus on breathing.

As soon as the elevator doors open, I make a beeline for my apartment.

Lyric.

My home.

She'll stop it. She'll help. She'll convince me I'm okay. That nothing bad is going to happen to me. That I wasn't followed.

What's wrong with me? Why can't I calm down? Why am I being paranoid? Was I followed? Is my mind playing tricks on me?

I open the door and softly close it behind me. My eyes won't focus. I sink against the door. I can't breathe. My heart won't stop racing.

"Lyric," I whisper.

"Mariah? Oh my God! Stay with me, baby!"

I feel her. I smell her sweet scent. But I can't see her. Everything is dark. My head is both heavy and light at the same time. It's spinning. I feel like I'm going to throw up. My whole body feels like it's underwater. My lungs burn. Like I'm drowning. Maybe I am. The pressure in my head is too much to bear. Lyric's voice is distant now. There's an inferno in my chest. I can't get enough air.

I feel myself fading, but I can't stop it. I can't stop the heaviness that envelops me as I slip into a deep, dark abyss. One I'm sure I'll never claw my way out of.

Not this time.

Chapter Two

☆ Lyric ☆

I fight the sobs threatening to escape as I try to be strong for my girl. Mariah has been fighting this panic attack ever since she got home last night. The takeout she brought home is still sitting in her car probably cooking in the Florida sun. Her car is going to need to be detailed, but that's the last thing on my mind right now.

"Mariah? Please, please tell me what happened. Who followed you?"

Mariah doesn't answer. Instead she sits curled up near the door with her arms tightly gripping her knees. She's been here all night. Just like this. She didn't sleep. Every time she closed her eyes, she started crying. She suddenly couldn't breathe again. It was like whatever happened on her way home from China 88 is something she's reliving over and over again.

I've seen Mariah have panic attacks before. We've been together for almost a year. But never have I seen her like this. She won't talk. She's shaking. She's crying. She comes down, and then it starts all over again as soon as she closes her eyes or moves. I'm usually able to calm her down. Usually if I hug her and stroke her hair and kiss her as I hold her close, she calms down. None of my usual tricks are working, and I'm fighting my own panic attack. The only thing keeping me going is the distraction of trying to help her.

Mariah and I met online a couple of years ago. I messaged her one day telling her how much I love her books. I didn't expect a response. Mariah already had a pretty large following on social media. I was really surprised when she messaged me back a few moments later thanking me for supporting her.

We started out talking about her books. It was surprising and so humbling to me that she appreciated my advice and was so open about her work with me. I was just a fan, and she was quickly becoming my favorite writer.

I looked forward to talking to her during the day, even though we lived in different time zones. She was in the United States, and I lived in the United Kingdom. It didn't matter to me, though. Talking to her was the highlight of my day. She made me feel respected and needed.

It didn't take long for me to start having feelings for her. I couldn't figure it out. I'd never been attracted to a woman before, but something about her… It didn't matter. She was married anyway. I didn't feel like I had a chance, even though her relationship was shitty. She'd opened up to me about more than just her books after a while. We became friends.

I resigned myself to believing that's all we would ever be. Until she opened up to me one day and said she was attracted to me and couldn't figure out why. She was just as confused as I was. She'd never been attracted to a woman before either. She was terrified to admit it, but she'd been feeling things for me for as long as I was about her.

As soon as we admitted our feelings for each other, I found myself imagining what it would be like to be together for real. On more than just text and chat. Mariah had planned to move away from her husband and start a life in Gainesville, Florida. It had been her dream to move to Gainesville for many, many years, even though she didn't know anyone. The two of us planned our move together. As soon as we admitted that we were so incredibly in love with each other, neither of us wanted to be apart.

I saved up to move to the United States. Mariah planned her move to Florida. She got there a couple of months before me, but helped me prepare everything I would need to make a move to the United States. Ever since I arrived, our life together has been perfect. Even though she suffers

14

from anxiety disorder with panic attacks, Mariah has always been a fighter, and I admire the hell out of her for that.

I run my fingers through Mariah's long, almost black hair and kiss her softly. Her eyes dart around the room. She usually closes them when I kiss her. My heart skips several beats and tears sting my eyes. I refuse to let them fall. I can't. Not when she needs me to be strong for her.

"Baby? Please talk to me..." I'd been pleading with her to tell me what happened for hours now to no avail. Instead of being able to soothe her, I feel like I'm losing a little more of her as the seconds pass. This has never happened. She's never been like this. She warned me it could happen, but Mariah has gotten so much better with her panic attacks.

"Followed... I was followed..." She's not even looking at me. I'm terrified because I don't understand what she's talking about.

"Who? Who followed you?" I try to get her to focus on me, but her eyes are wild. Like she's being hunted, and she's trying to stay ahead of the hunters. She looks at me briefly before she launches into an all-out panic attack again. It's all it takes. I wrap my arms around her trembling body and bury my face in her neck so she doesn't see me cry. "I don't know what to do, Rih." I shake my head into her neck as I kiss it. "I wish you'd talk to me. Please?"

"Followed..." Her arms are securely locked around her knees. She won't even attempt to hug me anymore. At least last night she could do that. She's becoming almost catatonic.

"I'm scared, Rih. I don't know what to do. Should I call for help?"

She slowly shakes her head and starts sobbing again. Guttural sobs. Like she's terrified. Her nails dig into her knees. "They followed me... Why?"

"Who?" I lean back on my knees keeping my arms around her shoulders. She's focused on the door to the balcony. I glance at the door for the millionth time wishing I had the courage to leave her for only a minute. I know she'll be safe here. We're on the top floor.

Across the hall is a police officer. One of our really good friends. Matt. Maybe I can get to him. I don't want to leave her, but I don't know what to do. If I call someone for help, they might take her to the hospital. She's so scared. The hospital might be her undoing. I don't even know where my phone is anyway.

He's a police officer. He'll know what to do, but… I hesitate after taking a few steps and turn back to her. I hate the idea of leaving Mariah. The problem is I don't feel like I have a choice now. I know when I'm outmatched, and I refuse to let Mariah suffer anymore. I need help. I need someone who might know what to do or can at least find someone who does.

"Mariah? I'm going across the hall. Okay?"

She doesn't answer. She just stares and cries and mutters. "Followed… Why? Why would they follow me? Who are they?"

I slowly get up, making sure she doesn't get too freaked out without me. I back towards the door, slowly opening it. I keep one eye on her and the other on the door across the hall. Maybe I should throw something at it. I eye the apple on the counter, but choose not to. Instead, I put a flip flop between the door and the frame to keep the door from closing just in case Mariah needs me. I quickly knock on the door and back up to stand next to ours with my arms folded across my chest.

When he doesn't answer, I nearly cry. I knock on it again, harder and a little more frantically, before jumping back to our door to listen to Mariah. She's still muttering.

I'm about to give up when I hear the lock on the door being turned. He opens it slowly and squints into the hallway. He sees me and leans up against the door frame folding his arms across his chest. He smiles tiredly.

"Hey, Lyric. What's up?"

"I know it's late or… early…" I shake my head. I don't even know what time it is. "I woke you, Matt. I'm so sorry. It's -" I bite my lip when Mariah sobs again. Matt looks over my shoulder and shifts, letting his hands fall to his sides. His muscles ripple with every movement, and I kick myself for thinking of how good he looks in those gray sweats and no shirt.

"You know my schedule. I know you wouldn't wake me if it wasn't important." He nods towards the sound of Mariah whimpering. "Is she okay?"

I shake my head. "She saw something last night. She came home…" I don't know how to finish.

"Panicking?"

"So much different than anything I've ever seen. I can't calm her down. Matt… I don't know what to do." I look down at the ground and jump at Mariah's cries.

16

"Do you know what happened last night?"

I shake my head. "She went to get takeout. She called me and said something happened to a police officer. When she got home, she said someone was following her. She hasn't stopped freaking out since then, and she can't get past saying she was followed. She keeps asking herself why."

"Why?"

"Why they were following her."

Something changes in Matt as he leans inside his door. He grabs something and closes it behind him. He crosses the hall to me and follows me inside. Mariah's head is hidden under her arms, and she's cry-screaming as she trembles. I immediately drop next to her and wrap her in my arms. Matt kneels in front of her.

"Mariah. Look at me," Matt says softly. Mariah shakes her head and continues cry-screaming as she rocks back and forth. I look at Matt completely at a loss as I hug my trembling girlfriend.

"Matt?"

"Ssh," he commands.

I bite my lip and immediately stay quiet. Why I suddenly feel a wetness pooling between my legs at a time like this is beyond me. I shift and rub my legs together a little. So stupid. What the hell is wrong with me? I internally berate myself.

Mariah. She's the focus right now.

"Mariah. Look at me. Now," Matt says with a dominant undertone.

"All I was doing was helping. Who were they?" Mariah mutters.

"Mariah," Matt says again.

"Who? Why me?"

"Mariah," Matt growls low and deep.

She looks up at him. I'm chilled to the bone when she looks right through him. Like she doesn't see him at all. "Why did they follow me?"

He takes her hands and untangles them from her knees. She grips onto his with a vice grip. "Mariah. Stop it."

"All I -"

"Mariah! Stop!" Matt's voice hits a level of dominance that sends both shivers and some kind of insane desire directly to my lower stomach.

I squeeze my thighs together and close my eyes. I've had feelings for him for a while. Mariah and I both have. But never have I had this kind

17

of a reaction to him. Nearly coming just from his tone. Mariah instantaneously stops and looks at him as she bites her lip.

"Good girl. Focus on me. Okay? You can do that for me like a good girl. Right?"

Mariah nods, and I force myself to keep looking at him so my mouth doesn't drop at how easily he's in control of her.

How easily he holds her attention.

"Keep looking at me, Mariah. Can you see me?"

Mariah nods and shakily reaches for his chest. She splays her hands across his chest and looks down. "I -"

"Mariah. Look at me. I didn't say look at my chest or your hands. Look at me," he says deeply. I can feel his voice vibrate through me. Mariah's eyes snap to Matt's at his command. I can't help myself. Mine automatically follow. "You're safe, Mariah. Do you trust me?" Mariah nods. "Do you believe me when I tell you that you're safe?"

Mariah nods again and whispers, "I believe you."

"Do you feel my heartbeat?" Mariah nods again, neither of us taking our eyes off Matt's. "Tell me what it feels like, Mariah. Do it now."

"It… feels… steady. Strong."

"Good girl. Breathe for me. Take a deep breath with me."

Mariah does as Matt says with no question. I find myself wanting to follow his orders just as much, but I force my focus to be on him calming down my girl. It takes only moments for him to do what I couldn't do all night long.

He reaches over and pushes some hair behind her ear. "Tell me what happened."

"I…," Mariah begins. "Was getting takeout. I… saw… an officer on the side of the road." She takes a deep breath, and I watch her nails dig into Matt's chest. I bite my lip and mentally slap myself for wishing my nails were hers.

"He needed help. You helped him. Right?"

"You… were there. You helped take my statement."

"Yes. What happened after you left?"

"I… called Lyric. I thought… I was being followed." She starts to sob again.

"Mariah. Stop. Now. You're not out there. You're here. With me. You're safe."

She bites her lip once more and forces herself to swallow the sobs. "I saw a black SUV. It followed me. I know it did. All the way here. They know. They know I live here." She starts to shake again.

I hug her tighter. "Honey, you're okay," I whisper in her ear.

"Say it, Mariah. Say you're safe," Matt demands.

"I… I'm safe."

"One more time."

"I'm… safe."

"You're safe. Good girl."

I deflate with relief. All of my tension and fear evaporates with every word Matt utters. His scent surrounds us; the room. It's calming. As calming as his commanding tone. His dominance.

Just as I think Mariah might be okay, there's a pounding on our door. Mariah opens her mouth to scream, but Matt is faster. Before any sound comes out, Matt's hands are immediately over both of our mouths. He gives us both a look, not a single word leaving his lips. We look at each other terrified and cower against the wall hugging each other as Matt slowly and silently stands. He steps to the door peeking through the peephole as the pounding continues.

"Jesus Christ," Matt growls as he opens the door. "What the fuck do you think you're doing, Cap?"

"I'm coming to talk to Mariah about last night. What are you doing here?"

"Calming her down. She was followed from the scene. Get in here, Brody. I know you know something I don't or you wouldn't be here."

The medium-sized, imposing, older man steps in. His eyes fall on us. Mariah and I are still cowering together on the floor. I don't know what exactly she saw, but whatever it was, Matt confirmed it. I'm scared to death.

Matt kneels down in front of us and holds out both of his hands. Mariah takes his hand slowly, and he effortlessly pulls her up with him as he stands. I bite my lip as I watch him reassure her.

My breathing quickens as my eyes dart from Matt's hand, to the intimidating man by the couch, to Mariah's back as she moves to the couch. I whimper almost silently, terrified because I have no idea what is happening right now. There's too much to process.

19

I'm frozen as my demon starts to taunt me. The being my mind conjured up to bring a face to all my insecurities and fears. *You're nothing but a burden. Your girl needs help, and you're useless. She doesn't need you. She has Matt to look after her. You do nothing but make everything harder for her. You should do them both a favor and dive off the balcony. You're no good. You're weak. You'll never be good enough for them.*

"Lyr-" I jump with a startled shriek and launch up, running for the safety of the bedroom, but I only make it as far as the kitchen before I stumble into the counter. Their shocked voices sound as if they are in a fog. My eyes dart around the room.

I close my eyes and lean my forehead against the counter. I mumble to myself and start to bang my head against it as I try to calm my racing heart and drone out the vicious snarl of *her.*

I can hear *her* laugh at me. *Do it harder. Maybe it will make you prettier. Better yet, maybe it will just end you. Then you won't be such a burden.*

"Lyric, shit! Stop it!" I hear Matt's dominant tone cut through her voice like a knife. One of his hands grips my arm. The other slides between my head and the counter, effectively stopping me from hurting myself. "Look at me," he whispers against my ear.

I look up at him with slightly wide eyes and a terrified squeak as I sniffle. "I -"

"Ssh... Listen." He slides between me and the counter, blocking my view of everyone and everything but him. His hands grip both of my arms. Hard enough to make me pay attention, but not hard enough to hurt me. "The biggest issue we have going on right now is that you have no clue what's happening." His voice is low and commanding. Dominant enough to cut through the bullshit in my head.

I nod slowly and stay focused on him. His eyes. They're so pretty. Like a golden brown. "Yes, sir," I whisper.

Something flashes across his eyes. Something I can't place. It's gone so quickly, I'm sure I imagined it anyway. He slides one hand slowly up my arm while keeping his firm grip on the other one. The wandering hand tangles in my hair. He keeps his eyes on mine as he pulls me closer to his chest. As soon as my ear hears his heartbeat, I melt into him and close my eyes. Then, and only then, do his arms wrap around me.

20

He rests his chin on my head and sways gently with me in his arms, slowly lulling me into a state of calm and serenity again. "Mariah saw a cop in trouble last night on her way home. She stopped because she couldn't allow him to get hurt. The guy he was fighting with got ahold of his gun. Mariah saved the cop's life last night."

"B-but s-someone f-followed her…"

Matt hugs me tighter. "I don't know, honey. If Mariah saw it, then I believe it. Brody is here because he has some information. I don't know what it is, but I want to find out. Don't you?" he asks me quietly.

I nod. "Y-yes, sir."

"There's my girl."

Gently and very slowly, Matt guides me to the couch. He doesn't let go of me as he leads me to our living room. He sits on the couch and pulls us both next to him. I'm always surprised at how natural and normal the action is. Sometimes, even though Mariah feels the same way, I hate myself for how good it feels to be in his arms. I love Mariah. With everything I am. I know she feels the same way. I shouldn't be feeling the way I do about Matt. It helps to know that she feels it, too. It's what I always go back on when my stupid demon tries to make me out to be a bad person.

I've felt this way for a long time. We both have. It's not hard to. The man is tall. He has to be six feet four at least. He's built of solid muscle. There's not an ounce of fat on him that I can see. Considering he isn't wearing a shirt, it's not hard to see the man is very keen on taking care of himself. And we both love the tattoos that snake up his arms.

But that isn't all. He's always checking in with us. He always says hi when he sees us. He always invites us over if he's barbecuing on his balcony. Lately, he's with us in some way every day, and we both really love it.

He's a flirt. We all flirt with each other all the time. Nothing has ever come of it, but we're all so easy with each other. We're all friends. I don't know when I really started to develop these feelings for him, but Mariah and I have had them for a long time. But how do two women the world views as lesbians, though we're both pansexual, not lesbians, tell the sexiest guy alive that they want him? And not just for sex.

Still, when he puts an arm around each of us, I could die happy. I don't miss how Mariah is completely calm now. He seems to have some kind of an effect on her. She's always been comfortable with him, but not like this. I don't understand it, but I'm feeling that same sense of safety. Peace.

I nuzzle into Matt as the man he called Brody sits on a chair across from us. Mariah has curled into a ball and is gripping the leg of Matt's sweatpants. I glance at him, always slightly shocked that he doesn't seem to mind how touchy-feely we can get.

I close my eyes and force all thoughts of him from my head. Now is not the time to be thinking about how his sweatpants leave nothing to the imagination. How being in his arms feels as natural as when I'm in Mariah's.

The feeling that nothing can touch me as long as she is holding me settles over me in this moment. I want to push it all away. To forget that I feel just as safe and loved in his arms as I do hers.

Mariah has made me feel all of this and more. I moved here for her. It may have happened quickly, but I fell for her within the first week that we started talking in the chat messenger. She loved me back when I was nothing more than a tired-out caregiver for my mother. When all I had to offer her was a minimal savings, which she cared nothing about, and my heart. She accepted and loved me in spite of it all.

She's everything to me.

My home.

But then, why does it feel like something is missing?

Why does it feel just as natural, just as... perfect with Matt?

Why do I feel like we need him just as deeply, just as profoundly as each other?

Chapter Three

☆ Matt ☆

I hug both Mariah and Lyric close to me while I watch Brody. Whatever information he has, I'm sure is going to piss me off. Since I'm pretty sure I know what it is, I refuse to let Mariah and Lyric be here by themselves while he tells them.

"Spit it out, Brody," I say dangerously. I know I'm being an asshole, but the idea that either of the girls I've considered mine for as long as I've known them being in danger has my blood boiling.

He looks at all three of us and sighs before shaking his head. "The guy last night. He was a member of the Eighth Avenue Gang. We have information from one of our informants that Mariah just made their hit list."

Mariah and Lyric both tense in my arms. I glare at Brody. "Couldn't have said that a little less aggressively? You have any idea what these girls just went through? Out."

"What?" Brody glances towards the door, then back to me.

"I said out. Go."

"Dude. I'm not done. She was followed by them last night. After I got done interviewing her. Remember when you watched her leaving and saw a vehicle pull behind her, but I told you it was nothing? They've been watching the building. They don't like that one of their guys was thrown in jail last night. They're looking for revenge."

Mariah gasps and sobs. She tries to get up, but I hold her tightly to me. Lyric has gone limp, like she's given up, as if she has no fight left in her. I can't blame her. Getting news like that, knowing your girl is in danger; that you can't protect her, isn't the easiest thing to hear.

"Brody. I can take it from here. I'm already kicking myself for not following Mariah home last night. Don't make me take that out on you by physically throwing you out." I can feel my chest tightening. I'm getting far more angry the more he talks, but it's more than that. I'm personally invested in this case. Mariah and Lyric have become very important to me. I've known them for about a year. I helped Mariah move Lyric in. I love being around them.

Lately, though, I can't go a day without them. Every day I'm not working, I make sure we all have dinner together. If I am working, I make sure I have lunch with them before I leave for the night.

"This is a problem, Matt. We need to get protection on her."

"Then do it. But do it from headquarters because you being here is scaring both of my girls more than you seem to understand. Both of these girls are just coming down from a panic attack, I'm not about to let you send them into another one. I'm not leaving either of them alone. I already didn't follow my instincts once. Fuck if I don't do it again. Get out. Let me deal with them. You deal with everything out there."

"Matt -"

"Brody. I'm not saying it again. I don't care that you're the higher ranking officer. When it comes to them, we do it my way."

Brody sighs as he stands. "Fine. I'll keep you updated."

"Wait!" Mariah says, jerking around to look at him. "What about DJ? How is he?"

Brody smiles softly. "He's okay."

I feel her visibly relax as she sinks into me. I look back up at Brody. "I want two squads patrolling this area at all times."

"You know as well as I do that we can't afford that."

"Then pull the State Patrol. Pull County. I don't care. Two squads."

24

He glares and mumbles something under his breath as he heads for the door. "I'll try to get it approved."

"I wasn't asking. Do what needs to be done. Or I will."

"Fine. I'll get it done. The department doesn't need you on another war path." Brody slams the door behind him not looking back at me.

I've never cared about him being my Captain. I don't take orders from anyone. Even in the military, I didn't take commands well. It's one of the reasons I rose in the ranks so quickly. In both the military and with Gainesville Police Department. I have a reputation for being a complete dick, but I could care less. I get things done, and the commanding officers eventually end up praising me for it.

Lyric shakily looks up at me. "You said your girls," she whispers.

I grip them both tighter but don't look at either of them. "I don't know when it happened, but I meant it."

Mariah burrows further into me. "Please, please don't let them get me."

"Mariah. I won't. I won't let them get either of you. I'll protect you. You can trust that as much as you trust me. And I know you trust me."

She shivers against me. I rub my hand comfortingly up and down her arm, keeping her firmly against my body. Lyric takes a deep breath and moves to stand, but I stop her.

She glances at me. "Now that we've started to come down, I need to get tea. She drinks a tea that relieves stress and calms her. I couldn't get her to drink it before."

I nod as I let her go. She hurries to the kitchen and turns on the kettle. "Lyric, when did this start? Her panic attack?"

She turns to me, chewing on her lip. "Last night... when she got home."

"Honey, don't let this kind of shit go on that long again. You should've called me or come over and woke me up long before you did."

"I thought I could handle it. I've never seen her like that before, though. I couldn't even get her to move. She was sitting on the floor all night long."

"Don't do this again. Don't let her suffer like that again. You should have called me, honey. I don't care if I'm working. I don't care if I'm sleeping after shift. I don't want either of you needing help like this

25

and not coming to me just because you thought I was too busy or didn't want to wake me up."

"I…" She looks down at her hands. "You're right. I should've come to you earlier," she says quietly. "I didn't even think to call. By the time I did, I had no idea where my phone was, so I just knocked on your door instead."

I glance down at Mariah, feeling her breathing begin to slow and even out. "Don't worry about that tea. Mariah is sound asleep."

Lyric's eyes widen. "How did you do that?"

I chuckle as I shift, gently lifting Mariah into my arms. "I think after she calmed down, she passed out. Can you open the door to your bedroom for me?"

Lyric turns off the burner and hurries ahead of me to open the door. She walks to the bed and turns down the covers. I set Mariah on the bed, careful to not wake her, before standing up. I give her a last look before turning for the door and motioning Lyric to follow.

"Are… you going to leave?" she asks me as soon as we're out of the room.

"Fuck no. Are you joking? I'm not leaving either of you. Fucking ever. I need to go to my apartment and grab some things, but I'm not going anywhere."

I watch as Lyric disappears back into the bedroom. I grab a set of their keys that they always leave in a bowl by the door so I can get back in. No way in hell I'm leaving this door unlocked for a second. Especially if I'm not behind it.

After locking their door behind me, I unlock my own door leaving it propped open. If there's any sound out there while I'm grabbing my stuff, I'll hear it and be able to investigate immediately.

I move through my apartment quickly, my mind focused completely on them. It's really nothing new. Those two have occupied my head ever since I first saw them, they were struggling to move a King-sized mattress into the building. It was by far one of the sexiest sights I'd ever seen.

I knew right away they were together, and fuck if that didn't turn me on even more. I know I'm not the only guy who has fantasized about being in bed with two women, but I might be the only guy who has claimed them both as mine long before either of them ever knew it.

After grabbing everything I need to be away for a few days, I walk swiftly back to their apartment, letting myself in and locking up behind me. I quietly walk to their bedroom, not seeing either of them in the main area. I silently let myself into their room. I don't care if I need to sleep in a chair. I'm not letting them out of my sight.

"Matt?" Mariah asks softly, turning to me.

I freeze. "Yeah?"

"I don't know why, but we feel safer with you close."

I put my duffle bag down with a half smile as I pull my gun out of the bag. "I'm not going anywhere, Mariah. I'll sit in the chair by the window. You both get some rest."

"Um... I meant like next to us. Like... in the bed, maybe?"

I glance at Lyric. "Is Lyric sleeping?"

"She couldn't stay awake any longer. I woke up after she came back into the room. We decided we needed to sleep. Lyric curled up with her arms wrapped around me just like this and hasn't moved."

"And she feels the same way? She would be okay with me in the bed with you both?"

"We both agreed. We'd like you to be with us. As close as possible. We feel safer that way. And... we... also... really like you... Like, a lot like you."

I clear my throat. My mind is racing with the intense feelings I have for both of these girls. I didn't fall for one over the other. I fell for both of them hard and fucking fast. I didn't know they felt the same way.

Over the past year, I found out both of them had been with men. Assholes who didn't treat them right. I thought maybe they decided to jump the fence because of it. Men hurt them, so they decided to give the opposite sex a try.

I couldn't have been more wrong about them, and that delighted the ever-living hell out of me, but they never admitted until right now how they felt about me. The attraction they both have for me is going to be fun to explore. They enjoy flirting with me just as much as I enjoy flirting with them, but I didn't know they had the same feelings as I do on the other side of it.

I've never taken it further because I didn't want to push them. I've never been like that. I've never spent so much time hiding my feelings and wants and needs from anyone. Then again, I've never felt so strongly for

27

anyone as I do for them. It's more than just want with them. More than desire. More than the idea of being with them. I need them. I've never needed anyone. I've never allowed myself to.

"I'll lay in the bed with you if you want, but I can keep you just as safe from the corner of the room." My voice cracks. My voice never fucking cracks. I'm nervous. I want to be in that bed with both of them.

Fuck, what's wrong with me? She's inviting me into that bed, and I'm hesitating. It's all I've wanted for a year, and I'm hesitating. I want them to be sure. As sure about me as I am about them.

"Matt," Mariah says softly. "Please?"

I close my eyes and mentally kick myself. I force myself to walk to the bed and crawl in. My intention is to take this slowly. To tell them both how I feel when they both are feeling better. I can't put it off any longer. I need to say more than just they're mine.

I set my gun on the nightstand, but I pause when Mariah pulls back the covers. My eyes nearly bulge out of my head and my traitorous cock is instantly hard. "Mariah. Are you not wearing clothes?"

"We don't really like sleeping in clothes. We feel like we're getting tangled up. Choking."

I back away, even though everything in me wants to crawl in next to them and pull them both close to me. "Mariah, you don't understand what you being naked next to me is going to do."

She chuckles softly. "You claimed us. Remember? You said we're your girls. You know we both really like you. I don't think we've been very good at hiding it."

I growl low in my throat as I look at the outline of both of their perfect tits down to Mariah's completely naked ass. "Mariah, I can't get into that bed with you without talking to you both about what we all expect out of this relationship."

It takes her a few moments to answer. So long, in fact, that I'm pretty fucking convinced I messed up. "Then lay on top of the covers if you want. Though, we don't want you to. We know what we want. And we know it's you. But please don't be far away from us."

I groan when she covers them both again. "Fuck it." I crawl under the covers and wrap both Mariah and Lyric in my arms. Mariah cuddles closer to Lyric, and I snuggle closer to her, burying my face in her coconut

28

infused hair and letting my hard on rest against her tight ass. My hand falls against Lyric's just as tight ass.

"Mmm…," Mariah murmurs, pushing against me.

I groan again. "Stop, baby. We need to talk about this. All three of us first."

"Don't need to… Already know…" She pushes against me again.

I inhale sharply. My dick begs to be out of the boxer briefs that I refuse to take off. "You're killing me," I murmur with a grin against the back of her neck.

"So is the fabric preventing me from feeling you," she whispers. She turns her head so she's looking over her shoulder at me. In the dim light of the room, I can see her perfect eyebrow raised.

"No fucking way. If these come off, I can't promise things won't get dirty."

She shrugs. I can feel the tease coming off her in waves. "Suit yourself." She turns back and burrows back into Lyric as she wiggles against me. My dick protests its confinement by attempting to shoot straight out in the most painful way possible.

"Fuck…," I groan. "You're a goddamn brat."

She giggles quietly and does it again, making me groan once more and press against her to relieve some of the pressure she's building. I nip her shoulder and kiss her neck. She lets out a quiet moan that makes my cock jump even more.

"Okay, okay," she whispers with a soft smile as she looks over her shoulder at me again. "I'll be good."

"Much too late for that, baby girl," I rumble low and quietly. I let go of Lyric carefully. I really don't want her to wake up. The girl is exhausted. I know Mariah is, too. Which is why as much as I want it to, this isn't going any further. "Go to sleep," I command as I take off the boxers.

"Okay… Stay."

"Not going anywhere, sweetheart," I whisper into her ear, pressing against her hard to selfishly give myself the pressure my cock needs. I hold both of them close and relish in the feel of Lyric's soft skin under my hand as I grip her ass, and Mariah's silky skin against my dick.

Lyric shivers a little bit and jumps in her sleep. Mariah snuggles her closer, wrapping around her tighter. I gently rub my hand up and down her thigh and hip, giving her sweet ass a soft squeeze as I let my eyes fall closed. The other hand tangles in her hair. Both of my girls are using my arm for a pillow. It allows me to hug them closer to me. I feel like they're more protected.

The more Lyric is soothed, the more her tension evaporates. "No go... Matt," she whispers. "We're safe... love..."

I smile. I don't know if she meant what I think she did, that she feels safe and loved with me, but I'll ask her about it later. Right now, the thought lulls me into a sleep I desperately need. "There's nowhere else in the world I'd rather be other than here. Right here with my girls."

★★★

It's hours later when I feel Lyric stir. I blink a few times and tighten my grip on her when I feel her start to pull away.

"Where are you going?" I ask sleepily. "What time is it?"

"Six. I was going to make dinner," she whispers.

"I need to clear the apartment first. Stay here." I reluctantly pull away from them and grab the gun I left on the nightstand when I laid down. I pull my boxer briefs on.

A person can never be too careful. I doubt anyone got in, but if I come face to face with someone, I'd rather do it without my dick hanging out.

I stealthily walk across the room and carefully open the door. I scan the open-floor plan apartment with my gun ready if I need it. Seeing nothing moving in the shadows, I breathe a sigh of relief and turn back into the bedroom.

"You're okay, but leave the bedroom door open."

"Sure." She smiles softly as she gets out of the bed.

I groan at the sight of her perfectly, perky ass. She turns slightly and stretches. Her arms rise above her head, and I get dizzy as all of the blood rushes directly to my dick.

Again.

"Lyric," I nearly plead.

"Hmm?" She looks over at me innocently. It's all I can do not to take her in my arms; show her how a real man treats a woman.

30

"Put some clothes on, or I won't be responsible for my actions."

She turns to me and gives me a sexy as hell laugh. "You have too much self-control not to be responsible for your own actions."

She's not wrong. I shake my head with a quiet chuckle. "Clothes. Now, Lyric." I sit down on the edge of the bed as she moves to the dresser.

"Yes, sir."

I inhale. Sharply. "Fuck," I mumble under my breath at the purely sassy way she said sir.

I force myself to keep my eyes off her, but it doesn't help. Instead, I decide to get dressed myself. Or at least put a shirt on. I grab my duffle bag and breathe a sigh of relief when she puts clothes on and leaves the room. I slowly slip my shirt on and crawl into bed next to Mariah. I wrap her in my arms and kiss her neck softly.

She moans and cuddles back into me. "Mmm... Matt..."

I smile into her neck and kiss up to her cheek. "Tell me you dream about me."

She shivers as I pull her closer. "All the time. We both do," she whispers.

I kiss the corner of her mouth as she pushes her ass against me. "I dream about you both all the time too." I gently graze my hand up to her incredible and full tits. I squeeze, and she gasps. I've wanted this for so long. Holding back isn't possible anymore. I need to touch her more than I need to breathe.

"I can't believe you want us."

"Are you okay with that?"

"I'm so okay with that... but..." She pauses with a sigh. "How is this going to work, Matt? I've never been in this type of a relationship before. Neither of us have."

"Neither have I, but we'll figure it out."

"I don't want anyone to feel left out. I'm so scared you're going to like being with each other more than either of you like being with me, but I've fantasized about this for so, so long. I -"

"Ssh... Not now. Get dressed. Lyric is making dinner." I kiss the corner of her mouth again and reluctantly get up.

Mariah sits up. The blanket falls around her waist as she stretches. I clench my fists and bite the inside of my cheek. Seeing her in a tank top wearing no bra is one thing. Seeing her in nothing makes me want to do things to her that are so dirty, it makes me want to take a shower. Things I just imagined doing to Lyric while she was prancing around here naked.

I tear my eyes away and make my way out to their living room as Lyric is putting soup into coffee cups. I chuckle as I sit on the couch. Mariah and Lyric are the only people I know who put soup into coffee cups, but it's one more thing I love about them. How different they are from anyone else. How neither of them give a shit what people think of them, or their quirks. It's the little things that set them apart and make them so ridiculously irresistible to me.

Mariah comes out as Lyric is bringing out the mugs of soup. Mariah efficiently grabs us all drinks, and I admire how they work so well together.

I watch as the two sit next to me. Lyric spreads a blanket out over us all, tucking it in around us as Mariah puts a movie on. They then curl themselves into me as the three of us settle in. It's not like we've never watched a movie like this before. Tonight, though, everything feels different. After opening Pandora's box into my feelings for them, there's no going back. Not like I'd even want to.

Chapter Four

✮ Mariah ✮

The movie we were watching ends, and I'm grateful no one decided to talk. We all just sat quietly enjoying the movie and each other. I needed to watch cute dogs trying to find their purpose. I needed to be held and comforted with no words at all. I hadn't realized just how much until Matt leans forward to grab the remote.

I'm instantly cold. I bite my lip watching him, but quickly look away and close my eyes, cuddling against the back of the couch, instantly missing him.

I blink a few times, focusing on Lyric. I smile softly when I see her eyes are on him, too. She really is everything to me. I love how shy she gets when I tell her how pretty she is, but how she takes what she wants. She's not shy about wanting me.

And neither of us are shy about our want of Matt.

Matt rests his elbows on his knees and sighs. "We all need to talk. This whole thing between us has gone on for long enough. I think it's time we're all honest with each other about what we feel, and what we expect and want from this." He keeps his eyes straight ahead.

Lyric and I look at each other.

It's Lyric who looks away first. She hates confrontation and isn't good about being the first to bring anything up in conversations like the one we're about to have. It scares her. I can't blame her, really. I'm scared, too. Even though I know how all of us feel for each other. It's just the question about how it's all going to work that scares us.

"You're right," I whisper with a heavy sigh.

Matt looks at me, then Lyric. "I'll go first." He sits back and tugs us back to his side. "First of all, I don't think any of us have been good about hiding how we feel about each other. I've had some serious feelings for both of you since I first met you. For me, this last year has been both the best and the worst of my life." He pauses, and Lyric and I both look down at our hands. "The best because I've had the two of you in my life. It's been… incredible. But it's sucked because I've kept all that I've come to feel away from the both of you because I didn't want to push."

"Same with us," Lyric says quietly.

"It's more than flirting. There's been many nights we've been just like this watching a movie or talking or playing a game, and I haven't wanted to let you go. I've never been in this situation before. I've never felt so strongly for anyone. Let alone two people. I've never let anyone into my life besides my family, and a couple close friends. But the two of you. I don't want to be away from you. I…" He shrugs. "I physically can't stay away from you any longer. I want it all with both of you."

I take a deep breath before looking at Lyric. I shift slightly and sit cross-legged next to him, looking at both him and Lyric. "I feel the same way." I say it quietly. "Everything with you and us feels so…"

"So natural," Lyric says, sitting up and turning towards me. She leans over and takes both of my hands as Matt's hands drop to our thighs. He rubs lightly. I'm immediately at ease. "I feel the same way." Lyric bites her lip and looks shyly between me and Matt.

"Look at me," Matt cuts in as he squeezes our thighs. We both look at him. "I don't want to get in the middle of what you have. If you aren't sure about the three of us all being together, tell me. I'll be honest in saying I'm not sure I'd be able to walk away, but I'll do it if you don't want anything to change."

I shake my head. "Lyric and I both want you, Matt. I… we… just have some concerns." I look down at mine and Lyric's linked hands. We decided if this talk ever came, I'd be the one to lead it. Lyric didn't think she'd be able to say what needs to be said. It's not in her nature.

"Now's the time, honey," Matt says quietly. He rubs both of our thighs soothingly.

I squeeze Lyrics hands but don't look up. "We don't want any of us to feel left out or the third-wheel. We both are scared that you're going to prefer one of us over the other and one of us will feel left out. Like, I know Lyric has more of a sex drive, if that makes sense…"

"Mariah. Relationships aren't all about sex," Matt says quietly.

I shake my head. "No, it's not just that." I can feel my mind racing as I try to explain all of our concerns. Not just mine. "I… I'm scared that you both will decide you love each other more than me. And that I'll get left out. Lyric feels the same way. That you'll prefer one of us over the other." Lyric tightens her grip on my hands. "What if… what if we're both having a bad day or something? And we both need you, or what if I need her, but you're too busy being with her, or you both get sick of me? What if -"

"Mariah. Stop. Now. Look at me." My eyes snap to Matt's at his command, and I notice Lyric's do, too. "Over the past year, have I favored her over you or you over her in any manner at all?"

I look into his beautiful coffee brown eyes and shake my head. "No…"

"Remember a few weeks ago when you were feeling really emotional, and Lyric was incredibly upset over something stupid her brother said to her?"

"Yeah…"

"Did I favor either of you? Or did I spend the entire day holding both of you close to me talking you both down?"

I smile softly. "You held us both close and spent the entire day making us feel…" My eyes widen slightly before I smile. "Loved. You made us feel loved. Cherished. Well, me at least."

Lyric smiles softly. "Me, too."

"If we do this," Matt starts. "If we decide that this is what we want, there's no going back for me. I already decided I can't lose you as friends. I need you, both of you, in my life. If we go through with this, losing either of you would destroy me. So this needs to be something we really think through. I don't want regrets."

I look at Lyric and can tell she's already thinking exactly what I am. I squeeze her hands. She smiles softly at me. She lets go of one of my hands and grabs Matt's. I follow her lead and take his other hand in mine as he watches us with curiosity.

"I think the three of us need to all be honest with each other," Lyric says softly as she looks at all of our linked hands. "Starting right now, no keeping anything from each other. We wouldn't have been so incredibly tortured this entire year thinking we were bad people for having feelings for someone we didn't think would return them."

"This won't work without honesty," I say just as softly as Lyric.

"No truer words have been spoken. It's important going forward that whenever one of us feels like something is missing, or if we need something, we speak up. We need to be sure that we're always being upfront with one another. And we need to be sure that if we feel this isn't working, we try to fix it. We don't walk away from each other. Relationships take time and work. This will probably take more, but I'm in this for the long haul. We all need to be."

Lyric and I look at each other for a long moment. Matt runs his fingers over the back of our hands. Finally, Lyric squeezes my hand. She brings it up to her lips and kisses it tenderly. "I really have strong feelings for him. Just as strong as they are for you. I know you know that already."

I blush. "Me, too." We both breathe deeply and look at Matt. "I'm in this. It's so crazy, but I… I want this. I never believed I'd be here, but I never believed I'd be with Lyric either. She was the best decision I've ever made."

"I took a huge step to come here. I was scared, but I did it," Lyric says. "This is a huge step, too, but…" She adorably bites her lip as she smiles softly and nods decisively. "This is right. I can feel it. I feel like this is where we're all meant to be. Where we belong."

I watch as Matt lets out the breath he was holding. "You have no idea how happy I am to hear you say that." He smiles as he relaxes.

I feel myself melting. "So…" I look between Lyric and Matt. "What now?"

"Now we treat this like we would any other relationship." Matt raises both of our hands to his lips and kisses them. "We've spent hours upon hours talking and flirting. Building up this tension. But you both went through a lot last night and today. We can't ignore that there's a huge threat out there."

I slump slightly. "I was hoping that it had all been a dream. That I'd wake up and everything would all be okay again."

Matt reaches up and touches my cheek. "I promise, Mariah. Nothing is going to happen to you. I won't let it."

I curl back into his side with a sigh. Lyric stands and leans over to kiss my cheek on her way to the kitchen. I watch her for a moment, thankful I made it home last night. Thankful my impulsive decision didn't get me or the officer killed.

"I can't stop going over it in my head. Every step. Everything I think I did wrong and could've done better."

Matt drops his arm back around me and kisses my forehead. "You saved DJ's life."

"I don't really remember you being there. I mean I do. But barely. Just that you asked a couple questions. The rest is almost a blur."

"I checked on you and DJ. After that, I dealt with the suspect. Questioning him. I led the scene investigation. I was still dealing with a few things when Brody released you from the scene. I almost called and told you to come back when I saw that vehicle pull out, but I ignored it. Brody said it was probably nothing."

"Yeah, if *nothing* consists of being followed home and thrust into the worst fucking panic attack you've ever experienced... then yeah, Brody. It's fucking nothing," Lyric says with a bit of venom in her voice.

"Neither of us did anything, Lyric," Matt says. "I ignored it. He thought it was purely coincidence."

"I still think it looked suspicious." Lyric shakes her head. "It doesn't matter. I wasn't there. So while I really don't know what happened, I do know you." She looks at me. "I don't think you did anything wrong." Lyric always knows exactly what to say. "You would have followed your instincts. They've never led you astray before."

"You haven't told her what happened?" Matt asks.

I shake my head. "I couldn't, Matt. I couldn't get the words out."

He takes a sip of his hot chocolate. "I think you should tell her. Now that you've calmed down."

I look up at him. "I don't... want... to go into another attack..." I sigh, though, because I know he's right.

37

"I'm right here. And so is she. But she needs to know what happened. All she knows right now is you were followed home by a gang member, and the cop from next door has made a vow to protect you. She needs to know the whole story."

I burrow into him. It takes me a few minutes to finally feel like I can do it. Matt's strength and Lyric's love give me the courage. Otherwise, I'd live with it buried deep inside me until I died. Just like I've done with so many other things in my life. Things I've never told anyone except Lyric and Matt.

I close my eyes and let Matt's fresh, spicy scent wash over me, relaxing me. "I was on my way home. I saw an officer on the side of the street. He was fighting with someone. I didn't really think. Instinct and training kicked in. I just acted. I rushed to them just as he was getting the officer's gun away from him. I took the guy down and grabbed the gun when he was stunned. I rushed back to DJ, the officer, and stayed with him. He was really hurt." I pause and squeeze my eyes shut. The memory, the fear, washes over me. I curl into myself.

Matt squeezes my shoulder and Lyric squeezes my hand. I hadn't even felt her grab it. "Matt and I are right here," she whispers.

It takes me another minute and another deep breath, breathing in Matt's cologne. "He taunted us. Tried to get up. I was holding him at gunpoint. He didn't think I'd shoot." I feel tears sting my eyes. I turn and bury my head in Matt's chest. "I shot. I shot the ground as close to his foot as I could without hitting him. It was like everything was going in slow motion. I saw the dirt spray up and hit him." I let out a sob.

"We got you, baby," Matt whispers into my hair as he runs his larger fingers through it.

"All I was... thinking was that I... needed to protect the officer. He needed to get... home. Just like me." I speak through my cries as the tears spill, soaking Matt's shirt. I squeeze Lyric's hand, trying to keep myself in the present and not get swallowed whole by the remembrance of the night.

"Oh, my poor baby." I feel Lyric shifting and moving, but I don't dare open my eyes. I'm not sure if I'll still be sitting on the couch in our living room. I might be wrestling some guy for survival on the side of the road again.

Suddenly, I feel Lyric pressed against my back with her arms wrapped tightly around me. Matt has shifted somehow and his warm, solid chest is shielding me. Both Lyric and Matt are wrapped around me like impenetrable walls. I turn and nuzzle Lyric's cheek as I bury myself in the safety of them both.

"You're okay, sweetheart. Can you feel us wrapped around you?" Matt's deep voice sinks into me, and I nod. "Nothing is going to happen to you. Nothing. Do you understand me?" I nod again. Lyric kisses my shoulder.

"I left the scene after they finished interviewing me. I called you, Lyric. That's when I noticed an SUV was following me. I thought I was being paranoid. So, I took random turns. But they stayed on me. I started getting scared. By the time I got home, I was trying to breathe, but I was so, so freaked out. I jumped out of the car and hid. They sped away. I ran into the building and couldn't hold on anymore."

"The panic attack overtook you," Matt says softly.

I nod again. "I kept telling myself to get to Lyric. She always makes it stop. But not even she could help. I thought I was going to die. I couldn't shut my mind off. I kept seeing them getting to me and Lyric!" I'm shaking. I know I am, but I can't feel it. I'm starting to not feel anything anymore. "No... not again... Please not again." My voice sounds distant to my own years.

"Matt! She's..." Lyric cries, but I can hardly hear her. Why is she whispering?

"Ssh, baby. I know. Let her go. Go to the bed and get it ready. Quickly."

Something envelops me, and I feel like I'm floating on soft clouds. After a few moments, I start to come down. My skin starts to feel cold. I shiver. All I can see is black. I'm wracked with sobs, but I can hardly hear myself.

"Rih, please, please stay with me."

"Lyric...," I whisper. I can feel her hair. Her soft skin against mine. I can't fade this time. I can't let the panic get me.

"Mariah. Listen to me, baby. You need to focus on us. Feel Lyric. She's pressed against your back. Can you feel our girl?"

Our girl.

Ours.

39

I focus on her. Her arms. Her lips on my shoulder. Her warm body against me. "Y-yes."

"Good girl. Can you feel me? Feel me wrapped around you?"

I force my fingers to move; to feel him. The ridges of his abs. His chest. I wrap my arms around him. Lyric hugs me even tighter as they both form a protective cocoon around me. "I feel you. I feel you both."

"We aren't going anywhere, Mariah. You're safe. No one is getting to you," Matt whispers.

I allow myself to relax as my eyes get heavy. "No one is getting to me."

"I love you, Mariah," Lyric whispers as she kisses me on the shoulder.

"I love you, too," I whisper back. I cuddle into both of them feeling safer than I've ever felt. My heart starts to slow, and my racing mind begins to calm. I drift off to the strong beat of Matt's heart, and the steady rhythm of Lyric's breathing.

Safe.

Protected.

Loved.

Home.

My Home.

Chapter Five

⋆ Lyric ⋆

(Two Days Later)

It's still dark when I wake up. I quietly slip out of the bed, careful not to wake up Mariah or Matt. I silently grab a pair of short gray shorts and a tight black tank top, slipping them on as I walk out of the bedroom.

It's been a couple of days since we all admitted our feelings for each other. I still hold so many fears. Things were perfect with me and Mariah. I'm afraid to think for a second that things could be just as, if not more, perfect with Matt now that we are all finally together. What if they decide they like each other better and don't need me anymore? What if they fall out of love with me? What if I make them angry and they decide I'm not worth it? I don't think I would survive if I lost one, let alone both of them.

I know it's crazy, but I wipe a tear away anyway as I open my laptop. I need a distraction from my thoughts. Sometimes they completely run away from me. I start thinking things that I should never think. Things that would never happen. Things that my heart knows would never happen in all of time.

I smile a little when I open up Mariah's latest book cover. I need to get the finishing touches on it before her release. We've changed it a hundred times and finally settled on something we both love. Now all that needs to be done is the text sizing.

I get lost in my work when it comes to helping my love. Mariah is always so humbled by everything that I do for her, and I'm awed by the work she puts into her books. I don't think I do much, but Mariah is always telling me how amazed and proud of me she is. The truth is, I enjoy it. I love being able to help her however I can.

I bite my lip and furrow my eyebrows as I tilt my head. If I can just get the color a little... no. Maybe a little lighter... I carefully adjust the color until it looks just right. I smile brightly at my screen mentally patting myself on the back. Mariah will love this. I love when she's proud of me. She lights up and looks so beautiful with the pride she feels.

"You know, you're beautiful when you get so into something you're passionate about." I jump and look up at Matt wide-eyed. He's standing against the door frame in nothing but his boxer briefs that leave nothing about him or his size to the imagination. His arms are crossed over his chest. Even in the dark, I can see how well-defined he is. The light from the moon spilling through the windows makes him look like some kind of God.

I bite my lip. "Um... I... didn't see you come out." I tuck a piece of hair behind my ear as I look down shyly. Matt uncrosses his arms and strides towards me. I watch him through barely raised eyes while he sits next to me. He puts an arm over my shoulders and pulls me into his side. I'm instantly comfortable and relaxed, though I didn't know I had been uncomfortable or anxious in the slightest.

"What's this for? It looks like a book cover. Something for Mariah?"

I nod as I cuddle into him. "She's got a release coming up. I needed to get this done. We try to get the paperback out before the eBook."

"Why? Why not release them at the same time?"

I furrow my eyebrows. "I don't really know, honestly. It's just something we've always done with her books. Her readers seem to like it. It's hard to gauge when the paperback will be approved so releasing it at the same time is difficult. Those who like the paperback seem to enjoy getting it early." I shrug.

"Just curious. The cover looks great. I'm always a little awed by how good her covers turn out."

I look up at him curiously. "Have you ever seen her books in print? They don't really seem like they're your... type."

He laughs softly. "They aren't. I'd never read romance novels before, but when I started getting to know you guys and found out she's a writer, I wanted to check her out. I secretly have all of her books stashed in my bedroom."

My eyes widen. "You do not!"

He smiles. "I do. She's a good writer. The covers are incredible. And now I know why."

"You knew I did all of this."

"Seeing it is different, though." He leans in to kiss me on the cheek. I smile. "So? Why are you up so early?"

"I don't know. I couldn't sleep. I woke up and started thinking about this cover. I couldn't get it out of my head."

"Is it finished now?"

"Mmhmm. What do you think?"

"I think you've outdone yourself. But I think that about every cover you do." He gently takes my laptop and sets it on the table in front of us before leaning back against the couch. He turns so he's facing me with his arm over the back of the couch. "I don't think that's everything, though." He drops his hand to my thigh and starts rubbing softly up and down moving ever so slowly to my inner thigh, while never taking his intense dark eyes off me. "Talk to me."

It's impossible to keep things from him, but I'm a little scared to bring any of my concerns up. Not doing it wouldn't be fair, though. And also not at all likely since he'd find a way to get it out of me. He always does.

I sigh and watch his hand moving lightly on my leg. "I'm scared that you and Mariah will start liking each other more than me. I'm scared you won't need me anymore."

"Lyric. We talked about this. You know how much Mariah loves you. How I feel."

"I know. I do. I'm... just being stupid."

43

His hand grips my thigh a little tighter. "You aren't stupid. I don't take lightly to you calling yourself stupid, and I don't like that you think that about yourself."

I nervously bite my lip. "I'm sorry."

"Don't do that again."

"I promise."

He goes back to lightly rubbing my inner thigh, inching his way higher as he looks at me. "It's not stupid to have fears in a new relationship."

My breath hitches when his hand stops just at my pussy. I swallow, silently willing him to go just a little higher. My hips involuntarily arch subtly. My throat gets dry. "Yes, sir." I barely hear the words leave my lips, but he must. His hand tightens on my thigh again. Only this time it's a little shaky. I hear him swallow. Hard.

"Lyric, don't call me 'sir.' You... don't know what that does to me."

"I... I'm sorry. It came out. I didn't mean -" He cuts me off with a hard kiss that brings a quiet moan from somewhere deep within. I close my eyes and melt into him. His tongue slips into my mouth and teases mine. He finally brushes his fingers against my already dripping, wet pussy. I fight myself on every level to not arch into him but lose the battle with epic ferocity.

His touch sends electric shockwaves through my system. I've been with guys before, but never one who nearly made me come just by running a finger over my pussy on the outside of my shorts.

He kisses down my jaw to my neck. I lean to the side to give him more access. He nips and sucks at my neck as he squeezes and rubs my pussy. The pressure building inside me makes my legs shake.

He sucks at my neck hard before licking it to soothe the sting. "Mine. Understand?" He squeezes my pussy again.

"Yours," I gasp.

His hand finds its way down my shorts, and before I'm fully aware what's happening, Matt is thrusting his perfectly large middle finger slowly and deeply inside my pussy. His lips find mine again. I close my eyes and let my hips move with him and his rhythm. I moan and pant quietly as we kiss, and he thrusts.

"Do you like that?" he asks, smiling against my mouth.

"Yes…"

He nuzzles my cheek. His stubble tickles my skin. "Yes, what? Say it, and I'll show you how fucking crazy it drives me."

My eyes widen as he thrusts harder; a little deeper. I kiss his jaw. "Yes, sir," I whisper in his ear. I moan quietly as he gives me another finger as a reward, filling my tight, wet pussy. I grip onto his arms as he quickens his pace. I'm so wet for him, I can hear myself. I've never been that way for anyone but Mariah.

"Good girl," he whispers as he kisses just below my ear. I lightly bite his shoulder. My hips move on their own as my pussy pulses and clenches for him. My nails dig into his arms.

"I'm… gonna…" I moan quietly again.

"Not yet. Slide your shorts down for me, my girl."

He continues thrusting into me deeply and hard. His fast pace never slows as I adjust just enough for me to push my shorts down. I tremble trying to follow his command and not come. My body wages a battle between wanting to please him and not come and wanting to please myself and come. In the end, my need to make Matt happy wins. I hold myself back.

"Oh, God… Matt… I… don't know how much longer…."

"Ssh…" He leans down and licks my clit. I throw my hand over my mouth to keep from screaming. The other tangles in his hair. He nips my clit and crooks his fingers inside me. My pussy clenches so tight around him, I'm sure he couldn't move them if he tried to. "Come for me, baby. Let me taste you."

"Mmm…," I moan into my hand.

My eyes roll back as my head drops against the couch. My fingers in his hair tighten as he sucks on my clit. I come for him so hard that I jerk off the couch. His fingers slide so deep inside me, my hips continue to jerk against him with the strongest orgasm I've ever had in my life. The jerking causes a second orgasm to hit before the first one is even done. My pussy pulses erratically. I squeeze my legs around his hand as he thrusts me through.

His slow rhythm helps me come down. Before long, I open my eyes and see him watching me with the cockiest grin I've ever seen. He stops his thrusts and pulls his fingers out slowly as my legs unclench from around his hand. I watch and bite my lip when he brings his fingers,

45

dripping with my essence, to his lips. He sucks me off of him. I nearly come all over again.

"You taste as sweet as I thought you would," he says huskily.

"Mmm..." I don't know what to say. All I can do is watch him as he sucks on his fingers. When he's done, he leans in to kiss me. It's not like I've never tasted myself on Mariah's tongue, but tasting myself on his is an entirely new experience.

He pulls back with a smile. "You okay?"

"I'm not used to..." I trail off shaking my head. I really don't know what to say; how to explain how I feel. I've been through so much... Things Matt knows, but doesn't know how I've been forever changed because of them.

"You're not used to being treated how a woman should be?"

I smile softly. "Not by men anyway."

He gently touches my cheek. "I'm not like them. I'd never treat you like them. I won't take what I need and leave you hanging, and I'll certainly never make you do anything you don't want to. None of them deserved you. Understand?"

I look up at him through my lashes submissively. "Yes, sir," I whisper.

He groans. "Lyric. That 'sir' thing is going to fucking kill me." He reaches down to adjust himself. I straddle him. He wraps his arms around me and pushes my hips down. "This. This is what you do to me."

I moan quietly and grind against his length, which is very impressive and really hard. "Mmm...," I moan again as I wrap my arms around his shoulders. I lean into him when he takes my lips with his again.

Dominantly.

I love how dominant he is. It's always called to my submissive side. A side of me I've never felt comfortable enough to show anyone but him and Mariah.

He groans into the kiss and pushes against me, but a knock at the door makes me jump.

I shrink into myself. "Who could that be at four in the morning?" I whisper.

"Shh!" Matt silently nudges me off of him and stands. He positions me behind him while he quickly walks to the door. He stops at our bedroom and glances in. Mariah is sleeping soundly. "Get in there. Go!"

46

He lightly shoves me into the bedroom and closes the door. I nearly run to the bed to wake Mariah.

"Mariah!" I whisper as loudly as I dare. She doesn't respond. "Mariah!" I don't whisper any louder, but I do start shaking her. "Mariah! Wake…" My eyes adjust to the dark. The curtains on the doors leading out to our balcony blow subtly in the light breeze. I look down at the bed and pull the covers back just as Matt bursts through the door.

"There was no one at that door. Where's Ma-" He stares horrified at the empty bed.

"I…" I can't breathe. No air is coming into my lungs.

Matt quickly looks around the room as he grabs his gun and phone. "Lyric. Take a breath."

"I…" I shake my head. I want to breathe, but the air isn't cooperating.

Matt takes my face in his hands. "Lyric. Sit down. Look at me." I do as he says and look up at him teary-eyed. "You need to breathe. You have to stay strong for me. I need to check around the apartment and call for backup. I can't do that if I need to take care of you. Fall apart later. Help me now. Please, baby."

I nod and focus on him as I breathe in deeply, getting needed air into my burning lungs. "Okay. Okay. I can help."

"That's my girl. Stay here. Don't move. Understand?"

"Yes." I nod and continue taking deep breaths. "Yes."

Matt holds his gun up as he starts checking the room. He checks the bathroom and closet as he dials a number on his phone. "Where the hell are my squads?" he barks into the receiver. "Well, she's gone, so they must not be out there!" Matt storms to the balcony and pulls the curtains back.

My eyes widen. I scream. "Rih!" I jump off the bed and run to the balcony. Matt catches me before I can get by him. Mariah turns towards me smiling. She takes her earbud out of her ear.

"Morning, my love."

"She's safe." Matt hangs up the phone and throws it onto the bed.

She looks up at him confused. "Is… everything okay?"

"Are you out of your fucking mind?!" Matt booms.

I cower, and Mariah looks at him dumbfounded. He steps forward and pulls her back into the room. He shoots a withering glare to the outside world as he slams the sliding door shut. He turns to Mariah, furious. I back

47

slowly away until my back is against the wall, and I'm hidden in a corner. I slide down the wall and make myself as small as possible, pulling my knees to my chest.

"Okay, I don't get it. Why are you so upset? And why are you holding a gun?" Mariah stands between Matt and me like some sort of soldier.

Matt looks down at his gun and growls. "Do you not have any idea what could've just happened to you? Mariah, you have gang members after you! There was just a knock at the door, but no one there! I walk into the bedroom and see the bed empty. The fucking curtains were blowing in the goddamn wind! It was like you vanished in thin air like in some stupid movie!"

Mariah crosses her arms over her chest and stares Matt down. "I have every right to walk outside without asking permission!"

Something very dark crosses Matt's face, and I involuntarily flinch. He looks like he's physically restraining himself from exploding. He shakes his head and crosses the room to put his gun away. "I don't know whether to spank you, or let you handle this on your own," he hisses.

"Stop acting like an asshole and talk to me like a person. How's that?"

"I've never allowed someone to talk to me like that. What the hell makes you think I'll start now?"

Mariah huffs and turns away from Matt. She starts walking towards the bathroom. "When you're ready to have an adult conversation instead of treating me like a child, we can talk."

I let out a strangled breath and slump back against the wall as the tension in the room seems to thicken. I tremble, hugging my knees tighter and watch Matt and Mariah from my chosen place on the floor in the corner.

He sighs as he puts his gun away and glances at me. "What are you doing?"

"I... hate conflict." I say it so quietly, I'm sure neither of them can hear me. I can't hear myself over the thundering in my ears.

"Honey, are you scared?" Mariah asks as she rushes to my side.

I can barely nod. My breath is coming out in short bursts of air, and I can't seem to take in enough oxygen to steady my breathing. My lungs feel like they're burning and might collapse at any moment.

Matt slowly walks over to me and kneels in front of me. I unconsciously cower back, watching him with slightly wide eyes. "Did I scare you?" he asks quietly. I nod hesitantly, not taking my eyes off of him. Mariah wraps herself around me and hums as she gently sways with me. "We've talked about this before. You know I wouldn't hurt you."

"But... you're really mad." I sob and grip Mariah's hair tightly.

"But did I lash out? Did I yell at you or strike you?" Matt asks. His voice is calm. Soothing, yet commanding.

I shake my head. "No..."

"Did I do anything to either of you other than walk away?"

"No..." I shake my head again. I loosen my grip around my legs as I slowly start to calm down.

He takes that as a sign and puts a hand gently on my knee, moving closer. "How many times have you seen me upset about something over the past year? How many times have I yelled but never anything more?"

"Um..."

He puts his arms around both me and Mariah. He hugs us tightly against his body. I melt into him feeling the last of my fear slip away. "My job is to protect you, Lyric," he whispers in my ear. "Take care of you. Love you. Not hurt you. I don't care how upset you see me get. I'm not like the guys in your past. I'd never do to you what they did. I'll never raise my hand to you. I'll never kick you or push you. I'll never scream at you. Say you understand."

I swallow a sob. "I understand."

"Good girl. I'm sorry I scared you, baby, but you have no reason to be scared. Not of me. I would never do anything to hurt you. Ever. There's nothing in this world that would ever make me hurt you. No matter how upset I get, I'll never harm you. I'll never stop loving you, Lyric." He kisses the top of my head.

"I know." His spicy scent fills me. Calms me. Mariah's silky, coconut infused hair that my face is buried in eases my out of control pulse.

"Forgive me?" Matt asks quietly, kissing my neck.

"Forgive you."

"Forgive me?" Mariah asks quietly.

I nod. "Forgive you. Always."

"That's my girl," Matt says.

49

"I'm sorry, Lyric. I know you hate when people yell and argue," Mariah whispers. She nuzzles my cheek before kissing my tears. She rubs her nose along mine and kisses me softly while Matt brushes away my tears with the pad of his thumb.

They hug me tightly until my body stops trembling, and my breathing returns to normal. I'm not sure how long it takes, but they don't let me go until I fall into a deep, exhausted, comfortable sleep.

Chapter Six

☆ Matt ☆

I check my watch and groan. Mariah locked herself in the bathroom as soon as we tucked Lyric into bed. I can't blame her. If I were her, I'd be pissed at me, too. I flew off the handle and scared the fuck out of both of them.

I look up when I hear the bathroom door in the bedroom open. I hear Mariah sniffle as she comes out, and I look down at my watch again. Three hours. She's managed to stay in that bathroom for three hours. I'm impressed with the girl's resolve.

I take a deep breath and stand up, slowly crossing the room to the bedroom door. I lean against the doorframe and watch her. She's managed to curl up in a tight ball on the bed next to Lyric with the covers over her head.

"You know, I'm not going away. No matter how long you hide from me. You may as well just give it up and talk to me."

"Not until you apologize for being an overbearing jerk." Her voice is garbled and hardly hearable.

"Jerk? A few hours ago I was an asshole. I'll take that as improvement." I smile a little hearing her chuckle softly. "Mariah, I won't apologize for protecting you. Maybe I should have told you everything so you understood what we're up against, but I didn't want to upset you. You know we're up against a gang, and you know how vicious this gang can be. I thought that would be enough."

She throws the covers off and shoots a withering glare at me. I might be a little intimidated if it wasn't so fucking sexy. She glances at Lyric, still sleeping peacefully beside her. She keeps her voice low, but I can hear the venom behind the words.

"Matt, you screamed at me! You grabbed my arm and yanked me inside with no explanation! You never told me I couldn't go outside onto my own balcony to get fresh air in the morning! I haven't been out of this house in a couple of days. Usually that doesn't bother me, but you know I love my balcony! You know I go out there every morning! And you know I haven't because I haven't been feeling well!"

I bite my lip to keep from smiling at her outburst, even though she's whispering. She's never been mad at me before. I never intended on making her mad at me, but the temptation is there if she's going to look that seductive.

"Mariah, when you decide you want to have a rational conversation about this, come out and talk to me. If you're going to throw a tantrum, stay in here until it's done. I'll tell you everything, but not if you're going to act like this."

Her mouth drops, and she reaches behind her for a pillow. "Ugh!" She throws it with all of her might at me, but I step aside and walk back to the couch without a backwards glance. I sit back down on the couch and wait.

After a few more minutes, Mariah comes out of the bedroom in a pink sports bra and a pair of black bootie shorts that match Lyric's. I try to stop myself from looking her up and down, but my attraction to her is just as strong as it is to Lyric. I wouldn't be able to stop myself if I tried.

Mariah and Lyric are both pretty similar in physical attributes. Both are small, petite women. Both have perfectly perky asses and large, very sensual tits. It's very difficult not to stare at either of them and fantasize about everything I want to do with them. Thinking that other men do the same damn thing, though, infuriates the ever living hell out of me.

I've been out with both of them over the past year plenty of times. Everywhere we go together, the two of them have men who can't take their eyes off them. I tried and failed on many different occasions to let them flirt and be flirted with because it's something fun they enjoy doing, but the possessive asshole in me always rears his head.

She softly closes the bedroom door behind her after checking once more on Lyric. "I started out being pissed at you for yelling at me. You know I don't like being yelled at. You know what I went through. You know I spent my entire life being berated by someone. My father. My ex-husband. What you did brought me right back to those days. I fought so hard to move on from that, and I won't go back. I won't ever let anyone treat me like that again."

Leave it to Mariah to put me in my place and make me feel worse than I already do. "I know. I'm sorry. I should've handled it better."

"What upset me the most, Matt, is that you scared Lyric. You know how she is. She's told you everything that happened to her. The way she was treated for years both through school and after with her exes. The bullying and the bullies yelling and kicking and screaming and hitting her. Her ex and the... you know." Mariah trails off.

She's never been able to say the word 'rape' when it comes to Lyric. Mariah herself was raped when she was a child by her step-uncle. She has no issue talking about that. Talking about what happened to Lyric, though, physically hurts her.

"You probably brought her right back to that day. Made her see flashbacks of everything that happened. You know she doesn't do well with yelling and conflict because of that. You know she does everything she can to make sure she doesn't upset anyone."

"I know, Mariah. I apologized to her. You were sitting right there when we talked."

"You shouldn't have done it in the first place." She hasn't moved from her place by the door to the bedroom. "She curled up in the corner while you were yelling at me. She cowered away from you. I wasn't facing her. I didn't see. Did you notice? Why didn't you stop?"

"Mariah. I apologized. It's all I could do."

"Don't you ever, ever do that again. You can scream and yell at me all you want to. I can take it, but don't you ever do it in front of her again."

"Mariah. Stop it. Now. Get over here."

"I don't really take well to demands."

53

She's starting to frustrate me. The problem is I can't figure out why it's such a turn on. "If you don't get over here, I'm going to take you over my knee." I give her a cocky smile as I cross my arms over my chest and lean back against the couch. *Come on, Mariah. Please. Challenge me,* I think to myself.

"I'm not a child."

"You're acting like one."

She stares me down. I tamp down every desire I have to give in to her pretty pout. Not the easiest thing I've ever done.

After a few moments of letting her have her fun in trying to get me to back down, I sigh. I get up and walk towards her. I waste no time in bending and lifting her, throwing her over my shoulder.

"Matt!" she quietly squeals in surprise. I slap her ass. Hard. "Hey!" I slap it again, just as hard. "Ow!"

I have to hand it to her. She's very conscious of Lyric sleeping in the other room. I turn and head back to the couch as she struggles to get free. "I warned you. I told you what would happen if you refused to listen."

"Put me down!" she whisper shouts.

I tug her shorts down, baring her ass, and slap it again. "I told you if you kept acting like a kid, I'd spank you." I slap her ass again just as hard as the first three times.

"Matt, put me down!" she yells quietly.

"No." I slap her ass hard again before sitting on the couch. I let her down enough so that she's straddling me but still not out of my grasp.

She glares harder at me. "Matt, let me go. This is ridiculous."

"Nope. You and I are going to talk." I wrap my arms around her and hold her firmly and close to my body.

Several minutes later, Mariah's body relaxes against me, and she lets out a sigh. "Thank you," she whispers against my neck.

"For what? A little while ago, I thought you might throw me off the balcony," I tease.

She laughs softly as she buries her face in my neck and tightens her grip. "I may have thought about it. But I like you too much."

"That's a relief."

"I'm sorry."

"Don't. You have nothing to be sorry for. I do."

"I shouldn't have been so mad at you and childishly locked myself in the bathroom."

"I should've been honest with you from the start about everything. I'm sorry for keeping things from you, and I'm even more sorry for upsetting you the way I did. I never should've lost control like that. The truth is, I was scared. We didn't see you in the bed. I saw the door open. I thought the knock was a distraction. I thought they came through the balcony and took you. When I saw you standing there, two thoughts went through my head. Neither of them were good."

She nuzzles my neck. "I'm sorry."

I tighten my grip. "I thought you'd been shot, Mariah. I thought you'd been propped up for us to find. Or that they tied you up and we're going to pull you over the edge as soon as I got out there. My mind was all over the place. When you turned around, I felt so much relief I almost wept at your feet, but I was pissed because I went through all of those emotions and thought all of those scenarios, and you were fine the entire time."

"I really didn't mean to scare you."

"You deserve to know the reason I was so scared in the first place. Maybe then you'll understand why I acted like that." I pause a moment as she shifts so she's pressed more fully against me. I kiss her shoulder softly and take a deep breath. "I got a text last night that they were outside watching. Patrol caught them. They took off. Patrol lost them, but they were out there. They were positioned in an area where they could see right into the bedroom. I don't know if that means they know what apartment you were in or if they were trying to figure it out, but I have to assume they know. I just got you and Lyric, Mariah. I don't want to lose you. I can't."

"I understand. If you told me that, I would've been more careful, but I didn't know. I should've thought about that, but I didn't. I'm sorry."

"It's done. Over with. I'm really sorry. I know you love your balcony, but I... can't allow you to be out there right now. I need to keep you safe, and I can't do that with you out in the open. It's going to drive you insane. I know it is, but I don't have a choice."

"I get it. Really. I do. I want to make sure I'm safe. I know everything you do is because you care."

"Rih, listen to me. It's more than just caring. I'm not doing this because I'm a cop, and it's my job. I'm not doing this because I care about people. This is personal to me because you and Lyric are my life now.

55

Now that the feelings are out in the open, and I've claimed you both as mine face to face instead of in my own head, losing you isn't an option for me."

I feel her smile into my neck. "I love when you say that."

"When I say what?"

"That we're yours. I never thought I'd ever agree to belonging to someone because I'm not a piece of property, but with you? I don't know… I know it isn't like that. I know you don't look at us like property."

"You aren't. I'd never think of either of you like that. You're my partners. The loves of my life, Rih. My heart belongs to you both. You and Lyric are the part of me I didn't know I was missing. I don't want anyone else, and I don't like the idea of anyone else having that opportunity with you. When I say you're mine, I mean I'm not willing to let you go without a fight. I'm going to protect you with everything I am. Just like I'm going to love you with all of me. I'm just as committed to you as you are me. At least I hope you are."

"You know I'm yours. You and Lyric make my life perfect. I fell so far in love with you in such a ridiculously short period of time, it scared me. It still kind of does, but I don't want anyone else. I'm happy with you and Lyric. Blissfully happy. I don't know what I'd do without either of you in my life."

"Does that mean you're saying you want to be just as much mine as you are Lyric's?"

"I'm saying I want all of us to be just as much each other's as we are to one another. If that makes sense."

"Perfectly."

She tightens her grip around my shoulders and presses herself tighter against me. I groan softly as my body immediately responds to her. She pulls back slightly, her eyes wide as she looks down.

"I…" She starts to scramble off me, but I hold her firmly against me, my length hardening by the second as she tries to stay still. She looks up at me again. "I didn't mean to… um… do that."

I chuckle. "I don't have an issue with it."

"I've never had anyone have that type of reaction to me. Well, except Lyric, but she doesn't have a dick."

56

I laugh. "Then you haven't been around the right type of men because you're gorgeous." I run my hand across her ass and down her hips, rubbing my thumbs against her thighs. I look at her and lean forward, kissing her. I kiss down her jaw and to her throat. My hands roam up and down her thighs. She gives me a quiet gasp, and her nails dig into my shoulders. I smile against her skin and flip her quickly onto her back.

"Oh!" She looks up at me in shock as I start tugging her shorts and panties down. "I've never…" She trails off and watches me. Her eyes shine a deep blue, and wonder reflects from them.

I kiss the inside of her thigh. "You've never what?" I look up at her, sliding one finger from her pussy to her clit and back down over and over as I watch her. She bites her lip and closes her eyes, subtly arching into me with every stroke.

She shakes her head like she's coming out of a fog. She opens her eyes just as I start making light circles around her clit with my thumb. She moans softly. "I've never… been touched… like this by… a man." She blushes a pretty bright red.

I give her a little more pressure to her clit and slide one finger inside her wet pussy. She grips the couch hard. "You've been with guys before." I give her lazy thrusts enjoying the way her body moves and responds to me.

"Not… like this. They never cared to touch me."

I slide a second finger inside her, and she arches into me. Her pussy tightens and clenches hard around my fingers. I can't believe how angry it makes me that the men she was with treated her so terribly. I don't understand how a woman like her could possibly have been married to anyone who didn't worship the ground she walks on. It only serves to make me pursue her pleasure more vigorously.

I thrust harder, faster, and deeper. She grips at anything she can as she meets my thrusts with every arch. She throws one hand over her mouth to keep from screaming too loudly as I crook my fingers inside her. I twist and spread them apart as I thrust. She tightens so hard around me that I expect her to come. Instead, she looks down at me and whimpers. Like she's begging me for permission but unable to say the words.

"Do you want to come for me, beautiful?" She nods. I flick her clit one last time and crook my fingers inside her again. "Come for me, honey."

"Mmm…" She closes her eyes and comes hard, collapsing against the couch and squeezing her legs around my arm. I kiss her knee as I thrust her through. She keeps her hand over her mouth and her eyes closed while her pussy pulses around my fingers.

One of the things I love most about Lyric and Mariah is their submissive nature. But it's not really only that. It's that they don't know just how submissive they are. Mariah waiting for me to give her the command to come seemed like the most natural thing for her to do at the time. Even though she'll argue about it and tell me that she isn't submissive at all. The fact that she does submissive things like that proves to me that she is.

As Mariah finally loosens her grip on me, I pull out slowly and kiss her thigh again. I pull her panties and shorts back up. I tug her up and sit on the couch next to her, sucking her sweet taste off my fingers. She cuddles into my side, gripping my shirt in her hand as she comes down.

"So, a guy has never made you come? Is that what I got out of that?"

She shrugs. "The guys I've been with have never cared enough to. The only people who have ever made me come are Lyric and myself."

"I'm shocked at the type of life you and Lyric led before you got together and came here. I feel like I have so much making up to do with both of you."

"You didn't do anything."

"No. But you both have missed out on so much. I can't wait to be the one that shows you all of it."

"It's not like we haven't been happy together, though."

"Honey, believe me. I don't doubt that you and Lyric satisfy every need the other has. All I'm saying is I think all of us are going to have a lot of fun together."

She laughs softly. "I knew it. That's all you want. To live out every guy's fantasy."

I know she's teasing, and I can't help but love her more for it. I run my fingers through her hair leaning down to kiss her forehead. She relaxes into me. Soon, her grip on my shirt lessens, and her breathing evens out. I look up as Lyric opens the bedroom door. She smiles softly seeing Mariah sleeping against me and makes her way to the couch. I hold my arm out, and she curls into my side, tucking her fingers into my waistband. I wrap my arm around her and pull her close, pressing a soft kiss to her forehead.

This.

This is what I've been missing in my life.

Them.

The loves of my life.

Chapter Seven

☆ Mariah ☆

(One Week Later)

I stare wistfully outside the large bay window in my living room. The sun is shining over Gainesville, but I can't enjoy it. I've been stuck inside for a week. This stupid gang has gone into hiding. I'm beginning to wonder if they are just a figment of all of our imaginations. Maybe the entire thing really was a dream. Maybe I woke up sometime and didn't realize it.

Matt hasn't left our apartment. He'd assigned himself to my case and put himself on bodyguard duty.

Case.

I hate the idea that I've become a police case. Like I'm just a number on some stupid file somewhere in the records room at the police station. I can't help but question if that's how Matt views me now. If the only reason he's stuck with us is because of this case.

Because I'm in danger.

Because Lyric is in danger because of me.

It's not that he's made me feel that way. Matt has been incredible. But I can tell he doesn't sleep well. He jerks awake in the middle of the night at the slightest sound. He checks the apartment several times a day. At night, he makes sure all the doors and windows are locked. And then he checks it a second time, third time, even a fourth. His gun is never not within his reach.

Lyric has withdrawn into herself. She's like an observer on the outside of the entire thing. She watches Matt. She watches me. But she barely moves from the couch or her chair. She mostly sits curled up in as tight of a ball as she's comfortable in, leaning against the arm of the couch or chair she's sitting in that day with her feet tucked underneath her. She hardly talks unless she's spoken to. Even then, we typically have to repeat whatever it was we said.

I sip my tea and stare out the window, trying to shake myself out of my thoughts. It doesn't work. I feel like this one decision has irrevocably changed the course of my entire life. Knowing this, would I have still stopped to help DJ?

I sniffle because I know myself. I know I still would've stopped. Even if I had been killed that night on the side of the road, I would've stopped. I couldn't leave an officer in need of help. Fighting for his life. I couldn't do that to anyone.

No. I would've stopped. And nothing would've changed. I'd still be in danger. A gang would still be after me. Lyric would still be terrified. Matt would still be protective. And I'd still be wondering if I fucked up my entire life and lost the only two people who I've ever loved so deeply, the thought of losing them is the most painful thing I can think of. My worst nightmare.

The only thing keeping me from falling completely apart is DJ. I needed to know how he was doing. I begged Matt to have him contact me. And he did. We've talked or texted every single day since. He's starting to become a good friend.

I jump a little when I hear Lyric's phone ring. She hasn't come out of the bedroom yet. It's nearly nine in the morning. Matt is laying on the couch with his gun on his chest staring at the ceiling. He hasn't said a word to me since last night. Not even a good morning.

I sigh and slowly stand, putting my tea on the table. I turn, spotting Lyric's phone on the counter. She must have left it there last night when

61

we went to bed. I cross the floor and grab it. The caller ID says unknown, so I don't answer it.

I've apologized to Lyric for putting her in this type of danger so many times over the past week that the words seem hollow at this point. Like there's no point in the words leaving my lips anymore. So I don't utter them. Instead, I've been staying quiet.

I glance at the couch as I set Lyric's phone back on the counter. Matt still hasn't moved, so I slowly make my way to the bathroom, my tea long forgotten, as I strip down and step into the shower. The tears falling intermingle with the water streaming over my body.

I stay in the shower until it turns cold. I don't realize that I've sunk to the shower floor somewhere during the time I've been in here. I'm not even sure how long it's been, but I crawl to the faucet and turn the water off.

Shivering, I pull myself up. I step out of the shower and grab a towel off the rack. I wrap it around myself and grab another, wrapping it around my hair. I take a deep, shuddering breath and walk back out to the bedroom. Lyric is no longer in the bed, and the bedroom door is closed. I thought I was all cried out, but the tears sting my eyes again. Before I know it, they're falling. I try to remain as silent as possible as I get dressed, but a quiet sob escapes.

After wiping my eyes and taking several deep breaths, I make my way back out to the living room, shocked to see it's nearly noon. Lyric is curled up in a chair by the window staring absently outside like I had been earlier. Matt is hunched over my laptop. Neither acknowledge me, and it makes me feel even worse for dragging them into this.

I walk to the kitchen, fighting more tears, and grab a glass for some chocolate milk. *Maybe I really am completely unlovable*, I think to myself as I pour. *I always manage to fuck something up.* I turn with my glass after putting the chocolate milk back in the fridge. I bite my lip and walk back to the bedroom with my head down. I sit down on the floor in a corner of the room keeping the lights off and the shades drawn, making it as dark as possible. Maybe I can just disappear.

I sip the milk as Matt appears in the doorway. He looks around the room, not seeing me immediately. "Mariah?"

I push myself further against the wall and close my eyes praying I'll vanish. I don't want to face anyone right now. I just want to be alone.

My luck, however, has never been good. I lucked out when Lyric admitted her feelings about me. I lucked out again when she actually moved here to be with me. My third time was Matt admitting he had the same feelings for both of us that we had for him. That's all the luck I dare dream to have in my entire lifetime since it's never been on my side before.

I can feel Matt's presence without opening my eyes. I sense when he kneels in front of me. When he touches my cheek softly, I whimper. I don't want him to stop, but I don't feel like I deserve it or him being so kind to me. Not since I dragged both him and Lyric into this stupid mess. I've ruined all of our lives.

"Don't, Matt," I whisper and shake my head. "Don't try and make me feel better out of some kind of guilt or anything. I know full well I deserve all of this."

His hand doesn't leave my cheek. "Deserve what?"

"You and Lyric mean the world to me." I open my eyes and try to move away from him. He's so big that I can't move far, though. All he has to do is shift, and I'm blocked. "I know you both are angry with me for ruining your lives. I understand."

"What are you talking about?" He looks confused. His hand drops to my knee as he looks at me. I look down.

"You should be working. You love your job. You haven't seen your family since this all started. I know they mean so much to you." I sniffle and grip my glass tighter. "Lyric doesn't deserve to be scared like this. It's my fault. If I hadn't stopped, everything would be perfect." I look back up at him. "And the worst part? I would do it all over again. I would stop to help DJ. I wouldn't learn my lesson."

"Mariah, you aren't making any sense. I think you have so many things going on in your beautiful mind that it's become jumbled. What's going on? Talk to me."

I take a deep breath and fight back more tears. "It's just that you haven't talked to me all day. You haven't been sleeping well the past few nights. And it's my fault because of this gang. They wouldn't be after me if I ha-" He silences me with a kiss. I'm so surprised, I stare at him wide-eyed as he pulls back.

"I'm sorry I haven't talked to you, honey. That has nothing to do with you. That has everything to do with me. I've been deep in my own thoughts trying to figure out a way to get you and Lyric out of here. I know you hate that you can't go outside for a walk or sit on your balcony. I know how much peace you feel in the morning on the balcony. It helps you to relax and helps you in having a good and productive day."

"I... thought you were mad at me. I thought you... I don't know." I shake my head. "Nevermind."

"You thought I what?"

I sigh. "That maybe you regretted telling us how you feel. And that I'm just a case to you. That Lyric got thrown into this mess and hates me."

"None of that is remotely close to being true. I've noticed how Lyric has withdrawn from us both. I can see how upset you are. I can see the guilt written all over you, and it hurts me to see it. I need to get you both out of here. I think I've figured out a way. Want to come out and see what I found?"

I sniffle as I nod. Matt takes my glass and sets it on the nightstand as he stands. He reaches down with both hands to help me up. I take them and he pulls me into him like I'm as light as a feather. He grabs my glass and keeps my hand in his as he leads me out to the couch. I sit next to him and look over at Lyric.

"Lyric? Want to come see Matt's idea on how to get us away from here?" I ask softly.

She glances over at me with the saddest eyes I've ever seen, but she gets up and sits next to Matt. She lets out a breath and looks at his laptop. I reach over for her hand. She takes it after a moment, and I breathe a sigh of relief. Matt leans over and kisses her cheek, then mine.

"There's some cabins in Otter Bay. It's about an hour away from here," Matt says as he shows us images of cabins for rent on his laptop. "There's a resort nearby, but one of the guys I work with has a cabin up there he barely uses. There's no people around for miles. No one would know we're there."

"So... we'll be alone?" I ask, afraid to dream.

Matt smiles. "Just the three of us. You'll be able to go outside. Get some fresh air. I still don't want either of you alone out there without me, but at least you'll be able to go outside."

I glance over at Lyric. She has a soft smile on her face, and her eyes have lit up for the first time in days. "Lyric?"

64

She looks at me. Her smile grows wider. "You mean we could just be by ourselves? No more hiding inside? No more being scared? Just us... being together?"

"Just us," Matt says. Lyric nods, just a little of her old, excited self coming back.

I look up at Matt. "Do you think maybe we could leave right now?" The thought of getting away from here is almost too good of a thought to push aside.

"Why don't you and Lyric get some things packed?"

Lyric and I excitedly get up and head for the bedroom. She's nearly bouncing. I'm nearly skipping.

Suddenly, though, a thought occurs to me, and I turn back to Matt. "Wait. What about them watching us?"

Lyric stands close to me, chewing her lip as we both look back at Matt.

"We'll go out in disguise, and we'll use a different vehicle. We can use mine. I doubt they know I have anything to do with you. And we'll go at dark."

"Disguises?" Lyric asks. "We don't have wigs, and we don't wear makeup." We both look at him, worried beyond belief. The butterflies in my stomach have taken flight. I feel like I'm going to throw up.

Matt stands and walks towards us. I can see the confidence in his eyes, and it sets me at ease. "Trust me." He stops in front of us, close enough that we can feel his body heat, and cups our cheeks in his large palm. "I know what I'm doing. It's not the first undercover operation I've run."

I nod and take a deep breath, leaning into his hand. "I trust you," I whisper.

He smiles and leans down to kiss me before turning his attention to Lyric. "What about you, sweet girl? Ready to do this? Do you trust me?"

Lyric nearly melts into him. I smile at the effect the man has on both of us. Lyric nods and nuzzles her cheek against his palm. "I trust you."

65

"Ready to get the fuck out of here?" Matt asks both of us. We each are wearing gym clothes with zip up hoodies. Lyric and I both have the hoods on the hoodies up. We're all carrying gym bags. Lyric and I both have our hair up and in a messy bun underneath the hoods. Matt thought making it look like we're just a few people going to the gym would draw little attention to us.

I reach over and hug Lyric. She's trembling and close to tears. "Soon, we'll be out of here. We won't have to be scared anymore," I whisper in her ear.

Matt folds us both into his arms. "I won't let anything happen to either of you. You know the plan. If we're followed, I stop at the police station, and we switch out vehicles with Brody. You guys hide in the back on the floor. Okay?"

We both nod, but Lyric is still trembling, and I realize all at once that she doesn't really understand what's going on and why.

"Matt? I understand what's happening because of my training," I say quietly as I look up at him. "She doesn't. She's never had the type of training and instruction that I have."

Matt nods as he pulls back slightly, keeping us both securely in his arms. "Lyric, honey. You understand why I want to leave, right? Why I want to get you out of here?"

She chews on her lip but nods. "Yes. You want to keep us safe and don't feel it's safe here."

"Good girl. In order to get you out of here safely, I have other officers patrolling the area. I have the entire SWAT team hidden out there looking for anything I don't see. I have DJ out there. We know there's people out there watching for Mariah. Right?"

Lyric nods again. Her grip on my side tightens, and I lean in to nuzzle her. "I know. I just wish I could do something to protect her. I feel completely helpless."

Matt tugs her hair and kisses her forehead. "Right now, the only thing both of us can do to protect our girl is to get her out of here. We have to trust in my team and my partners, in DJ, to help us get her out of here. Understand?" Lyric nods again. "Good girl. As soon as we get outside, we need to get to the truck as quickly as we can. Can you do that for me, sweet girl?"

Lyric takes a couple deep breaths and nods before kissing both of us lightly. "Let's go. I'm ready to leave all of this behind and spend time with you both. I feel like we need the time to regroup and be with each other."

Matt pulls back and opens the door. He checks the hall and leads the both of us out. We all breathe a collective sigh of relief when the doors to the elevator close.

Matt looks down at us. "We need to act like we're having a good ole' time. Three friends going to the gym. We need to talk, laugh, and act like nothing is wrong, like we don't have a care in the world."

Lyric and I both nod as the elevator doors open on the ground floor. We follow Matt outside, sticking close to him but following his directions. Lyric and I laugh, acting like Matt said something hilarious. Matt's head isn't on a swivel, but I can tell he's looking around. He's tense. His body is coiled like a viper, ready to strike if he needs to.

Lyric and I continue to smile and laugh as we hurry to Matt's truck. He grabs our bags and puts them on the floor in the back. He helps us into the front seat of his truck. I can tell he's fighting hard with himself not to look all around. He's putting a serious amount of trust in the officers we all know are in the area watching as we flee.

As soon as the both of us are in the truck, Matt closes the door and hurries to the driver side. He breathes a quiet sigh of relief that I know Lyric can't hear. I send up a silent prayer for that. She's already nervous enough. She doesn't need to see Matt is, too. Matt is the anchor for both of us right now.

I wrap my arms around Lyric as Matt drives. He reaches over and squeezes my thigh, then Lyric's before he focuses back on the road. He drives us as quickly as he can out of Gainesville and towards Otter Bay. The lights from the city fade behind us.

67

Chapter Eight

☆ Lyric ☆

I blink sleepily awake to the feel of Mariah running her fingers through my hair. I smile softly and tilt my head, nuzzling her hand.

"I miss waking up like this," I whisper. "It's been too long."

Mariah cups my cheek and leans down to kiss me. "I know." Our lips meet, and I melt into the kiss. Our tongues meet in an explosion of passion that we've both been without, and my body is instantaneously alight with desire for my girl. My nipples turn to peaks hard enough to cut glass as Mariah tightens her grip in my hair and presses herself against me.

I moan into the kiss. Mariah climbs on top of me, straddling me and pushing me down into the bed as she deepens the kiss. Our tongues fight for dominance. When she pulls back, I look around quickly for Matt, suddenly curious where he is. I don't get the chance to ask, though. Mariah starts kissing down my jaw and neck, making her way to my tits. I gasp and arch, tangling my fingers into her hair when she nips me.

"Mmm…" I writhe under her sudden assault on my breasts. Her tongue takes turns licking and sucking each nipple furiously. She squeezes and plays with the one her tongue isn't ravishing. I'm so wrapped up in what her tongue is doing, I don't notice that her hand is between my legs until she thrusts two fingers hard and deep into my pussy. "Fuck! Mariah!" I arch almost off the bed and completely submit to her.

She giggles. "I love when you do that."

I tug her hair. "When I do what?"

She thrusts faster, and I spread my legs wider. She nips my nipple before she starts kissing down my stomach to my wet and quivering pussy. "When you arch off the bed like that because it feels so good."

She nips my clit. My hips jerk into her mouth. "God... Mariah..." I moan and writhe under her as her tongue circles my clit. Her fingers hit the perfect rhythm. The one that drives me so crazy for her I can't remember my own name.

She giggles again. "I love the way you taste."

My eyes roll back into my head, and I pull her head harder against me as her tongue finds the perfect pressure against my tiny bundle of nerves. "Please... don't stop. Don't stop... Don't stop!"

She hums against my clit and crooks her fingers inside me as she twists them, thrusting hard. She licks down to my pussy and slides her tongue in with the furious pace of her fingers. "Mmm..."

"Mariah! Oh!" It's all it takes for me to lose complete control of myself and come hard on her waiting tongue, arching and moaning her name. I collapse against the bed, panting and gripping the sheets; her hair. She slows her thrusts as my hips jerk against her. My pussy clenches and pulses around her fingers as I come down.

She slowly pulls her fingers out and closes her eyes as she sucks me off of them. I moan softly as she opens her eyes and gives me a sexy smile as she looks up at me. "I love when you come undone."

I sit up and tug her onto her knees. I crush my lips to hers, tasting myself on her tongue, as I push her onto her back, not breaking the kiss for a moment. I give her no warning. No teasing. No fingers. Nothing. Instead, I shift and dive into her pussy with my tongue. I close my eyes, savoring her sweetness. Mariah bucks against me with each swipe of my tongue. Each hum. Each moan.

I shake my head back and forth vigorously, my tongue following my movements as I suck and nip at her pussy, driving her insane with need. I know Mariah. I know exactly how to pursue her pleasure; to make her writhe and moan for me; to make her lose control. I know if I keep

69

doing exactly what I'm doing, she'll come hard with a scream. It's one of my favorite sounds and sights in the entire world.

"Lyric! I... I'm gonna..." She pants and writhes. I hum into her pussy, nipping her as I pull back and blow cool air on her pussy. She comes hard as I thrust my tongue into her again, sucking hard as she pulses around my tongue. "Oh, God! Yes!" She grips the sheets and arches into me as she pulses. "Oh, God..."

I kiss up her stomach to her tits. I nip at each of them as she looks down at me and giggles. She runs both of her hands through my hair. When I reach her lips, she pulls me down and kisses me passionately. Deeply. We melt into each other with our limbs tangled around each other.

★★★

About an hour later, Matt's hand slapping my ass wakes me up. I moan and shake my ass. Matt laughs. "As sexy as the two of you look tangled up like that, it's almost noon. You both need to eat something, and we need to talk."

Mariah sighs and looks up at him. "About what?"

"Lots of things. We can start with you thinking this is all your fault, and Lyric feeling helpless. I made a chicken salad. Clean up and get dressed." Matt slaps my ass again. I bite my lip as I look up at him through my lashes. He doesn't see, though. He disappears quickly out the door, very obviously adjusting himself.

"That man is seriously beautiful," I whisper.

"You're telling me. It isn't fair."

"It should be a crime to be as attractive as he is."

"A felony. He should spend life in prison."

I laugh as I kiss Mariah softly. I slowly get up and start heading to the bathroom. Mariah shifts and follows. "His sentence should be him cuffed to our bed. We'd be able to ride him all we want."

Mariah cracks up as we both walk to the bathroom. "Whenever we want."

After we're cleaned up and dressed, we walk out to the kitchen hand in hand. Matt is leaning against the counter with his phone to his ear.

70

He hangs up when he sees us. I raise an eyebrow. Mariah goes stiff next to me, tightens her grip on my hand, and swallows hard.

Matt shakes his head. "I was checking in with Brody, baby. Nothing happened." He leans down and kisses both of us.

He takes mine and Mariah's free hands and leads us to the couch in the living room. He has three bowls with a salad prepared for us with three glasses of milk. He sits us down, settling between us. The news is on the television in the background. The sound is low so as not to bother us.

I smile as we all dig into the lunch Matt prepared. Before Mariah, I'd never had anyone care about me. I've always been the one to take care of everyone else's needs. No one ever really cared to take care of me or my needs. Simple things, like making sure I eat, or making sure I'm okay if I'm quiet or emotional. Now, Matt cares just as much as Mariah does. It's something I never believed anyone would ever do for me before. Now, I have two people who care as deeply for me as I do them. Who love me as much as I do them.

I smile softly to myself as I take all of our dishes into the kitchen after we've finished our salads. I quickly clean up, watching how incredibly cute Mariah is cuddled contently into Matt's side. When I'm finished, I grab a glass of orange juice for each of us and walk back to the couch. I put the glasses on the table and cuddle into Matt's other side. I tuck my fingers into his waistband, reaching my other hand across his lap to rub Mariah's thigh as I lean my head on Matt's broad, rock-hard chest. Matt pulls me into him, tucking me just as much into him as he has Mariah.

"First and foremost, I think we need to talk about how you feel like this is all your fault, Mariah. How did you come to feel that way?" Matt asks softly. Mariah looks down at his shirt as she holds it in her hand.

She bites her lip and curls up as much as she can as she shrugs. "I feel like it is my fault. If I hadn't stopped and helped DJ, Lyric wouldn't be scared. You'd be working instead of being on bodyguard duty." She doesn't meet either of our eyes. She continues playing with Matt's shirt. "I feel guilty because I know the consequences, but if I had a choice to go back and live it all over again, I would make the same choice. I feel like a horrible person because it caused all of..." She looks around the room before cuddling back into Matt's side. She grips his shirt tighter as she breathes deeply a moment. "This."

71

"Mariah," Matt says quietly. I give her thigh a gentle squeeze. She looks at me tearfully with a trembling lip, but doesn't quite make it up far enough to look at Matt.

"I'm so sorry," she whispers, looking at me. Her tears start to fall. "I'm so sorry that I got you into this. That you're so scared. I wouldn't blame you if you hated me..." She hides her face in Matt's side, and my heart breaks. I lean over and kiss her cheek softly as she trembles. I reach up and touch her cheek.

"Rih, it's not that I've been scared. I mean, I am. A little. But that isn't everything, and I certainly don't hate you."

Matt tugs Mariah's hair gently, forcing her to look up. "Honey, look at us."

She peeks up at me and Matt. "You don't hate me?" She sniffles.

I shake my head. "I could never hate you." I lean over and kiss her softly again. "Were you really living this last week thinking I hate you?

She nods. "I thought you both were mad at me. Neither of you touched me. When we went to bed, you both were so cold to me. You barely talked to me or acknowledged me." She looks down again and starts chewing on her lip.

I bite mine hard. Tears sting my eyes when I realize I made her feel even worse. "I didn't mean to make you think I was mad at you," I whisper.

"Mariah, honey, I know you and I discussed yesterday that me being quiet had nothing to do with you. I'm sorry it came off as if I was ignoring you. I didn't mean that. I really was trying to think of ways to keep you safe. Especially after finding out they were watching your place. But I never hated you. I don't." He leans down and kisses her forehead.

"It's just that... I..." She shakes her head. She lowers her voice. "You both know that I need to be held or touched when I'm upset or need to be calmed down. Neither of you did that even though you always have since I've known you..."

My heart ties itself into a knot at the pain Mariah is admitting she's been feeling. Knowing I've been a part of making her feel that way is like a knife being stabbed right into my chest and twisted. I never wanted to make my girl feel like I was mad at her or hated her.

"I'm so sorry," I whisper with a sob. "I didn't think about you feeling like that. I've been so upset with myself because I couldn't do

72

anything to help protect you…" I pause as I grip her thigh and Matt's waistband tighter. "I didn't feel worthy of being close to either of you."

"What? Lyric why would you feel like that?" Matt asks. I shrug, and he takes a deep breath tightening his grip on both of us. "I don't ever want either of you feeling like that. Mariah. Lyric. You both know better. You both love each other. This situation sucks. It really does. Things happened over the past week that aren't typical things that happen to people in real life. That's not your fault. You did the right thing. From this day forward, though, we need to move past that."

Mariah takes a deep breath and nods. She reaches down and squeezes my hand. "He's right. We can't do this anymore. You can't feel like you aren't worthy. And I can't feel like you hate me over events that weren't either of our fault. We can't hold back with each other. None of us can. No matter if it upsets us. This won't work any other way. And I won't risk losing either of you. Not for anything."

I look down at my hands as I chew my lip. "I just feel like I don't have the same experience you both do. I feel like I don't have the skills to protect Mariah if anything were to happen. I sort of feel like a failure because I don't know all the same things you both do when it comes to self-defense. I never went through the training that you both did. I feel like I'm not good enough or strong enough to protect you, Rih." I sniffle and choke back a sob, trying to stay strong. "I feel like I don't have anything in common with you, Matt. I don't have that law enforcement bond that you and Mariah have. I feel like eventually you both will get tired of me being a burden on you because I feel like I'm weighing you down."

This past week has served no other purpose than to make my mind run wild. I've always taken comfort in the small touches. It's one of the reasons Mariah and I get along so well. She's the same way. It's also one of the reasons Matt gets along so well with both of us. He doesn't mind either of us being touchy-feely with him. I understand why Mariah felt the way she did, thinking me and Matt hated her. I get it because I'm just like her. I need that sense of touch. I need to be held. Just like her.

Being with Mariah this morning eased some of the fear I've been battling that she doesn't want me. That I'm not good enough for her because I can't do anything to protect her. But I still have that niggling voice that I can't quiet. That stupid little voice that makes me think not only does Mariah not want me, but that Matt doesn't either.

Matt chuckles, and I look up at him, confused. Mariah tilts her head, curiously. "There's a very easy way to solve that problem," Matt says.

It's my turn to tilt my head curiously. He leans in and kisses me tenderly before turning to Mariah and kissing her just as sweetly as he had me. "What do you mean?" I ask, reaching up to wipe a tear away.

Matt uses the pad of his thumb to dry my eyes. "I mean this is private land. There's no one around for miles. I have a few guns with me. I took extra ammunition because I already had this idea before we left." He glances at Mariah, then back at me. "Mariah goes with me every weekend to the range to keep up with her skills. It's something you never expressed interest in, so I never offered to take you. I wish you had, but it doesn't matter now."

I watch as Mariah's eyes light up, and her confused expression turns to sudden understanding. I furrow my eyebrows, not following. "What doesn't matter now?"

"We could teach her how to shoot and fight! It could be really fun! Something we could all do together," Mariah says excitedly.

My heart leaps a little at the prospect of finally being able to learn at least a small fraction of the things they do. "Really?" I ask quietly.

Matt smiles. "Yeah. Really. But that doesn't address your biggest problem."

I look down sadly, biting my lip with a sigh. "Yeah…"

"Lyric." Matt gently cups my chin and lifts my face to meet his beautiful brown eyes. Mariah reaches over and runs her fingers through my hair with a soft smile. Her eyes shine with unadulterated love and adoration. "Honey, your lack of confidence in yourself is astounding to me. You thinking that there's nothing about you that would keep us interested in you, or that we have more in common with each other than you is crazy."

"Babe, I've been in love with you since you first messaged me. You're so funny and smart and so, so talented. You love reading with me. You love brainstorming with me. You love watching movies with me. You hate wind and loud thunder. You love watching storms because it's peaceful, minus the wind and thunder, of course. You can't sit there and tell me that we have nothing in common." She tugs my hair, and I smile

74

softly, lowering my lashes when she leans over and kisses me on the cheek.

"There's so much to love about you, beautiful," Matt says. "I love that you love movies and music. I love that you love learning. I mean, what kind of woman learns about American football just because the guy she has a thing for doesn't miss a game? I love being able to have conversations with you about anything and nothing. I love watching you work on Mariah's book covers. I love watching you design. I love watching you concentrate. I love how you can get me out of my head."

I blush a furious shade of some color I'm sure they haven't come up with a name for yet. "So you... won't get sick of me?"

"Hey... Lyric, I've been with you for a year. Have I gotten sick of you yet? I can't get enough of you!"

"Honey." Matt kisses me softly. I look up at him through my lashes. "It's impossible to get sick of you. There's far too much to love."

I smile softly. The tension in my body at the thought of them not wanting me anymore slowly dissipates as Matt pulls me and Mariah close to him. Mariah links our fingers together, kissing my hand before resting our hands over his lap. The longer he hugs us, the more relaxed I feel.

When he's satisfied that Mariah and I are both feeling better, Matt lets us go. He leads us outside, and he and Mariah spend the rest of the day teaching me moves the two of them learned in school and on the job. Before the sun sets, I've managed to break out of numerous holds and put both Matt and Mariah in several of my own. After they finish teaching me the basics, they start showing me the basics of shooting a handgun. By the end of the night, I feel far more confident about defending both myself and our girl.

There isn't anything I wouldn't do for Mariah, and now that I've learned ways to keep both of us safe, I start to feel more worthy of her love. I start to feel more confident that Matt finds me as loveable as he said he does. The place in this relationship that I wasn't sure I had, starts to become more visible to me. I slip into it hesitantly, but I'm far more confident that it is, indeed, my place.

Chapter Nine

☆ Matt ☆

Waking up laying in the middle of Lyric and Mariah with them wrapped around me has become my new favorite thing. I live for mornings like this. Mornings where I know the two of them are safe and happy in my arms where they belong.

I smile at the feel of their silky smooth skin pressed against me. Their soft and supple tits brushing my skin. Their legs thrown over mine as they cuddle into me. Their fingers linked together with their palms resting over my heart. Them snuggled into my side is like nothing I've ever felt or want to again. Them not liking wearing clothes to bed is a benefit I'm really enjoying.

I shift slightly and drop my hands to their sides, resting them just on the side of each of their tits. The movement causes both of them to blink awake and make the cutest sighing noise I've ever heard as they nuzzle my chest. Also one of my new favorite things.

They both kiss my chest and look up at me sleepily. Their natural beauty, large curious eyes, and perfectly kissable lips do things to me no woman has ever managed to do. I've never wanted anyone as much as I do them.

I hug them tighter to me. "I love you. Both of you."

Lyric's eyes tear up, just as they always do when I tell her I love her, as she leans up to kiss me softly. She pulls back, and rubs her nose along mine. "I love you, too, Matt. I don't know when or how it happened, but I do."

I kiss her again. "You deserve it. You deserve it all." It's something I always say to her. She's gone through a lot and doesn't believe she's worthy of love. She's getting there. Day by day.

Mariah hides her face in my chest. I know she's blushing, even though I can't see it. I tug her hair lightly. She looks up at me, just as teary as Lyric had been. "I'm so in love with you, too, Matt." She says it so softly, I almost can't hear. Her eyes light up, just as they always do when I say those words. She shyly kisses my cheek. I can't help but chuckle.

They both smile softly up at me before giving each other a look that I can't decipher. It looks suspiciously like they're plotting. What, though, has me baffled. I narrow my eyes as I watch them.

Without a word they both start kissing down my chest. They each nip and lick a nipple simultaneously, and I don't know whether to be impressed at how in tune they are with each other or scared shitless that they can speak without words.

They continue slowly kissing down my chest, continuing to my stomach. They lick and suck along the ridges of my abs. I can do nothing but give a breathy moan. My hands fist in their hair on their own. I have no control over my actions anymore.

"Fuck…" My eyes want to close, but the rest of me wins out. I want to watch. It's not like they haven't sucked me off before. We've just never been together like this. At least not yet. I've been waiting for them to be ready. Taking things at their pace.

They both giggle and continue kissing down my stomach to my hard as fuck and impatient dick. They both lick my tip, pulling back to blow cold air over it. They kiss each other over it, licking it and nipping lightly. I arch into them involuntarily.

Or maybe voluntarily.

Fuck. I don't even know.

Lyric closes her eyes and licks down my shaft to my balls. "Mmm…" She takes each of my balls into her mouth in turn and sucks gently, tugging on one then the other as she splits her attention between them. Mariah scrapes her teeth softly over my tip before taking it into her mouth and sucking hard.

"Holy… fuck…" My mind nearly goes blank with the dual sensations, and I can't figure out how I'm able to speak at all. Maybe I hadn't. Maybe that was all in my mind.

"Mmm…, Matt," Mariah hums against me as she pulls away and licks down my dick. Lyric takes her place sucking on my tip while Mariah nips and sucks her way down to my balls giving them the same attention Lyric had. I shake my head to clear the fog as they both start pumping my dick together.

Before I can react, Lyric takes me as far into her mouth as she can until I'm buried in the back of her throat, sucking hard as she hums and swallows around me. Mariah still strokes me as she sucks on my balls. Lyric pulls back slowly, scraping her teeth along my dick. My grip tightens on both of their hair. My arms shake. My dick throbs. I arch up as Lyric takes me back into her mouth. Mariah sucks hard, tugging on my balls, and strokes my cock while Lyric sucks equally as hard on my tip.

I try to tug them both away when I feel myself get close, but I'm far too weakened with pleasure to do any such thing. As if they can sense I'm on the edge and about to fucking jump, they both pull away, and concentrate on my tip, licking, nipping and sucking, as they each wrap their hand around me, stroking firmly. My eyes roll back, and I come hard as soon as I feel both of their tongues touch each other's tongue as they're licking me.

They both moan and take turns taking me in their mouth as I come. They suck and swallow everything I give them, then lick everything up that they don't catch. I spill my load into both of their mouths, completely out of control of my own movements. My hips rock up with every pulse, and my body jerks.

"Fuck! Lyric! Mariah!" I've never screamed a woman's name before. Let alone two of them. They're the only ones who have had that honor. I've never come so explosively before. I've also never been tag teamed by anyone before. My mind has never blanked out like that. So all I can think of is what's happening to my dick.

It takes me a few minutes to come down. I hadn't realized that somewhere during the time I was coming, I had closed my eyes. When I finally feel myself coming back to myself, I open them slowly. Grinning

78

up at me are my girls with the sexiest smirks I've ever had the privilege of seeing on anyone. With their chins resting on their hands, their hands resting on my thighs, both of them are looking up at me like they know they did well, but they want, no, need the confirmation.

As an answer I slowly sit up. I flip Lyric onto her back, then Mariah. I give them both a cocky smile and tug them closer to each other. They look at each other before looking back up at me, biting their lips. I put Lyric's leg over Mariah's, straddle them, and lean forward. I kiss the inside of each of their thighs and nip each of their pussies. They shiver and arch with a low moan.

I give each of them a few long licks from their pussies to their clits. They tremble at my touch and take each other's hands, twining their fingers together as they watch me work. I dive into Lyric's pussy with my tongue.

She arches into me with a yelp as I nip her. "Fuck! Matt!"

I bury my tongue inside her and my face against her. My tongue takes on a mind of its own, swirling and thrusting fast and hard in pursuit of her pleasure. She arches with a low moan and grinds against my tongue, gripping the pillow behind her. I nip her again and hum against her, sending vibrations straight into every pleasure nerve she has. I pull back just as I feel her start clenching hard around my tongue. She whimpers and looks down at me with the sexiest pout.

"Patience," I say deeply as I nip her clit. She jerks as I move over to Mariah. She looks at me shyly, but with wide, sexy doe eyes in anticipation of what's about to happen. I glance at Lyric just as she licks her lips while she watches.

I dip down and give Mariah the same attention, unable to stop myself from diving into her just as hard and fast as I had Lyric. She tastes just as sweet and responds just as sexily. Her hips jerk into me as I nip her pussy.

"Oh, God! Matt!" She pants. I suck and lick and swirl my tongue inside her. She grinds into me. As I feel her start to clench and pulse, I pull back with a nip to her clit. "Mmm…" She looks at me curiously as I reach a hand down to her and tug her up.

I can't see it, but I know my eyes are on fire with desire and need. "Straddle her face," I command.

79

Mariah inhales sharply as she nods and does what she's told. "Yes, sir."

She has no idea that all of the blood in my body rushes directly to my dick when either of them call me 'sir.' I watch with heavy eyes as she straddles Lyric and faces me. I position myself on my knees between Lyric's legs and look at Mariah.

I smile and lean forward to kiss her. "Lyric?"

"Yes, sir?"

"Lick her. No fingers."

"Yes, sir."

"Good girls." I don't give Lyric any warning as I plunge my cock into her. I watch with an odd sense of pride as she plunges her tongue into Mariah's already ready pussy with a low moan.

"Oh, fuck!" They both cry out in unison. Mariah grips her thighs and grinds down onto Lyric's tongue. Lyric arches into me, wrapping her legs around my waist, as she meets every hard deep thrust I give her, clenching around my dick. Her hands grip at the blankets as she moans into Mariah's pussy sending vibrations straight through her, making her arch and cry out in pleasure.

I watch as she hums into Mariah's pussy, sending Mariah into a near frenzy. My girls definitely know how to play with each other. I grip Lyric's hips and lift her higher off the bed so I can bury myself deeper inside her. Every clench and pulse drives me to near madness. Her constant moans cause me to drive into her harder, deeper, and faster until there's no way I can hold on any longer.

"Matt…" Mariah looks at me, pleadingly, and I can tell she's as ready as Lyric and me are. I can tell she won't be able to hold on much longer. I can feel Lyric is about to lose complete control. Her frantic thrusts against me and licks against Mariah tell me everything I need to know. I watch as she nips Mariah's clit. "Lyric! Oh!"

Mariah throws her head back and almost collapses against me. Lyric slams just as hard against me as I'm slamming into her. Her thighs are starting to tremble as hard as she's clenching and pulsing around me. Every fiber of my being is screaming for a release that I don't know I'll be able to recover from.

"Oh, fuck! Come for me. Now." My dick throbs and aches. Lyric clenches hard around me as she screams and arches off the bed, ripping my release from me.

"Matt! Oh, God, yes! Matt!" Lyric's shouts are muffled against Mariah's pussy, the vibrations causing Mariah to jerk and moan as Lyric doubles her efforts to make her come, shaking her head as she sucks and nips.

"Fuck! Lyric!" My eyes roll back in my head as I bury my dick deep into her pussy, pulsing as I shoot my load inside her. I come harder than I've ever come in my life. I shake and shiver against her as my dick uncontrollably thrusts into her. I grip her hips as she clenches and pulses, her hips jerking as she takes me even deeper.

"Oh God, yes! Lyric!" Mariah collapses as she comes while Lyric greedily licks and sucks at her.

I catch her against me as I force myself to thrust slower into Lyric. Mariah's entire body jerks as she comes with soft sighs and moans. I tangle her hair around my fist as we all pant while we come down. I thrust slower and slower, forcing Lyric to come down with me. She moans softly as she licks Mariah clean. She kisses Mariah's clit and pulls away licking her lips as she looks up at me shyly and bites her lip.

After a few minutes of all of us regaining a little of the strength we used, I slowly pull out of Lyric. She moans sexily. I move from between her legs and help Mariah off her. I look down at Lyric and decide to test my theory. I know both of them are submissive to an extent, but I think Lyric is far more submissive than Mariah.

"Get in your submissive position," I command as dominantly as I can over my racing heart.

I've hidden that side of me for many years, not wanting to give in completely to it. Not feeling safe enough to let it totally out.

To my utter shock and total delight, Lyric scrambles up and kneels. She straightens her back and puts her hands on her thighs, sitting back on her heels. Her legs are slightly spread for me. She looks up at me through her lashes giving me the perfect submissive look to go along with her perfect submissive pose.

"Fuck me," I whisper more to myself than for anyone else to hear.

Shaking myself out of the sexual haze I just put myself in imagining everything I could do to her, I turn back to Mariah. Sensing she would never be able to take me nearly as hard as Lyric, I lay down and guide her on top of me. I know how big I am. I also know from talking to them and learning about them over the past year that Mariah has only ever been with two men and neither of them ever gave her what she needed. Her experience compared to Lyric is levels below.

Not to say Lyric has been with that many men. She hasn't. But she's been far more sexual with them than Mariah has. I once asked Mariah how many times she's had sex, and her response was that she could count the amount on two hands. She'd never told me how many that was, though.

I didn't need to know. I had all the information I needed just by that one statement. I guide Mariah down slowly onto me. Her eyes widen. She bites her lip as she squeezes her eyes shut.

I stop. "You okay? I know I'm bigger than anything you've had."

She shakes her head. "You're bigger than anything Lyric has had, too," she whispers.

"People are different. She can take more than you can because she's experienced different things."

She takes a deep breath. I feel the moment she relaxes enough for me to slide further and further inside. I look over at Lyric, making sure she's still following my directions. My eyes widen slightly when I see her bite and lick her bottom lip. Her eyes are zeroed in on my dick and Mariah's pussy as I slowly enter her, and fuck if that doesn't make me harder.

When Mariah takes me as deeply as she can, I slowly start thrusting. She becomes wetter and wetter, becoming slicker for me. I thrust further and further until I'm balls deep inside her just as I had been with Lyric. I slide my hands up her thighs to her ass, guiding her up and down on top of me, matching her to my slow pace. She steadies herself by splaying her palms over my abs.

Her soft moans and needy sighs bring me closer and closer and she pulses and clenches around me. I can tell Lyric is just as turned on as me. She's trying to hold her pose, but I've seen her shift, spreading her legs wider. She's gripping her thighs so hard I can see the marks from her fingers. Her pussy is dripping wet, and she's started subtly moving her hips, mimicking Mariah's movements as she watches my dick slide into Mariah's tight pussy.

"Don't move, Lyric," I demand. She immediately stops moving her hips with a soft whimper. Her lips part further, and she grips her thighs harder. I fear she may draw blood.

"Oh, Matt..." Mariah lets her head fall back as she meets my rhythm. Her chest pushes out, and her tits start bouncing along with her as she slides herself up and down my dick. Before long, I feel her start shaking and trembling. Her pussy tightens around me and pulses. I grip her ass hard, forcing her to stop moving, and I bury myself in her.

"Come for me, sweet girl," I command as I look up at her. She comes so hard she can't hold herself up. She collapses on top of me and her pussy squeezes my dick just as tight as Lyric had. I didn't think it was possible to come just as hard as I had with Lyric again, but I do. I come hard holding Mariah tightly as we both jerk with every pulse. "Oh, fuck! Mariah!"

"Yes! Matt!" Mariah screams, digging her nails into my chest as she trembles, clenching around my dick. She gasps and pants as she lays sprawled on top of me. I continue to slowly thrust as she comes down. Lyric whimpers again, and I turn to her. I slowly pull out of Mariah and shift her off me. I sit up and tug Lyric towards us.

"Oh!" she cries out, shocked. I kiss her deeply as I lay her down on the bed. I kiss down her body, stopping to nip each of her nipples.

She grips my hair and tugs lightly as she arches into my mouth. "You were such a good girl, sitting there watching like that." I nip her tits again.

"Ah!" She jerks into me. I look up at Mariah and cock my head, signaling her to me and Lyric. She smiles softly, eyes hooded, and crawls to me. I move to one side of Lyric with Mariah on the other. We both lean down and start lavishing Lyric's tits and nipples. "Ah! Oh... Matt... Mariah!"

She tangles her fingers in both of our hair and writhes underneath us, trying to pull us both down harder against her. I nip her nipple and start kissing down her body. Mariah follows.

When we reach her sweet pussy, I give her a long lick from her clit to her pussy and pull back. Mariah follows my lead and does the same thing, nipping at Lyric's dripping center. I grin when Lyric inhales sharply and bucks her hips into us. Mariah pulls back and kisses Lyric's thigh while I slowly slide my tongue into her pussy.

"Oh… Fuck! Matt!" Lyric cries out.

"I love how you respond to me," I say. I thrust my tongue into her again. Mariah leans down and starts licking Lyric's clit. She hums against it, and I feel her pussy tighten and start to pulse around me.

"Mariah!"

I smile and swirl my tongue inside her. She arches and starts bucking her hips to the fast and hard rhythm I set. Mariah moans against Lyric's clit at the same time I hum into her pussy. Lyric screams and clenches hard.

"Mmm… Lyric…," Mariah says in a sing-song voice.

"I'm gonna…!"

I nip her pussy and blow cold air on it. "Come for us, beautiful."

"Ah! Fuck! Matt! Mariah!" She grips the sheets and arches nearly off the bed, but I grip her hips and hold her firmly down. She comes hard, bucking against my grasp. Mariah nips her clit and does the same thing I did. She blows cool air on her.

Lyric writhes and gasps as she pants and continues coming. Mariah and I both lean down and lick her clean as she comes down. She tries to close her legs at the overwhelming sensation, but we stop her, each sliding a hand up her thighs and spreading her legs. No way we're missing how sexy she looks when she comes.

When she finishes, she collapses against the bed. Mariah and I both kiss our way up her body until we reach her lips. We both kiss her, then cuddle her into both of us. Mariah wraps her arms around Lyric. I wrap my arms around both of them.

"I love you," Lyric whispers, cuddling into my chest, and tightening her grip on Mariah's arm wrapped around her. "Both of you."

Mariah smiles softly and nuzzles Lyric before looking at me. "I love you both, too."

I kiss both of them tenderly. "I love you both more than I can express."

No more words need to be said as the three of us lay there, enjoying each other after the euphoria of the love-making we just shared.

Before long, my girls are so relaxed, they fall asleep. Wanting nothing more in the world than to be with them, I follow into a peaceful slumber with them tucked safely and securely in my arms.

Chapter Ten

☆ Mariah ☆

I'm not really sure what time it is when I wake up. Truthfully, I don't really remember going to sleep. What I do remember is this morning. I smile to myself as I gently untangle myself from Lyric and Matt. Matt stirs, and I pause, making sure I don't wake him up.

I glance out the window as I quietly get out of the bed and stretch. It has to be around noon. The sun is so bright and high in the sky. I grab my phone and walk to the bathroom. After I've cleaned up, I make my way back to the bedroom. Lyric is stretching sleepily and Matt is sitting on the bed rubbing his eyes.

"Fuck. I wasn't intending on going back to sleep after that. It's already past noon," Matt drawls. I've noticed that his Southern accent is more prevalent when he's tired or just waking up. I can't help but shiver and bite my lip. I see Lyric shiver and hear her moan softly. I'm pretty sure he doesn't realize how sexy his accent is. Or what hearing it does to us.

"I think this morning's workout may have worn us out," I say shyly. Lyric giggles and kisses his cheek before crawling out of bed, heading for the bathroom, pausing to kiss my cheek on the way. Matt watches her for a moment then looks back at me, giving me a panty-soaking smile.

"I've been waiting for that for longer than I care to admit to," he says raspily.

I blush and try to hide it as I get dressed, but I can feel his eyes on me. I clear my throat. "My new book is being released in a couple weeks. I need to finish my edit." I take a deep breath after I pull my tank top over my sports bra.

"I was thinking of maybe taking Lyric outside and teaching her more defensive moves. She's got the shooting down, but she could use more practice. I was hoping you'd help so it's more than just me. I want to get her over her apprehension of hurting people."

"Oh…" I bite my lip, still avoiding his eyes, knowing I need to get to my edit.

However, the fact that Lyric feels the way she does when it comes to being able to defend herself, and me if the time were to arrive, makes my decision for me.

When it comes down to it, Lyric is the most important thing to me. If she feels like this is something she needs to do, I'll do anything I can to help.

I nod and brave looking over at him. "Okay. I think that's a good idea. Should I set up the targets for shooting? Or do you just want to walk her through more defensive moves?"

"We can do night shooting with her later after the sun goes down." Matt stands and stretches as he yawns. His back is to me, and I inhale sharply.

His muscles ripple as he reaches over his head. I let my eyes travel down his back until they reach his perfect ass. I linger. I barely even register him turning around, but before I know what's happening, I get a full frontal view of his sculpted body. The tattoos that run up and down both his arms make his muscles look impossibly larger… firmer. His abs look like they're chiseled from granite. His sexy V drags my eyes directly to his beautiful cock.

He grins. He knows exactly what he does to women, but especially to me and Lyric. "Like what you see?"

I involuntarily lick my lower lip, incapable of looking at anything other than him. "Looking like you do should be outlawed. You should arrest yourself."

He rewards me with a deep laugh as he cockily strides towards me. He leans down and captures my lips with his just as the shower in the bathroom turns on. I moan when he deepens it. His tongue teases mine. He takes a handful of my ass in each of his hands and jerks me towards him. I completely melt against his body, breathless. I surrender to him and his kiss, having no other option.

When he finally pulls slowly away, I sway against him. I have no recollection of putting my arms around his shoulders or digging my nails into his shoulder blades. It takes me a full minute to chance opening my eyes and looking up at him.

"God..."

He runs a thumb over my cheek. "You okay?"

"I think I forgot my name..."

He kisses me softly again before whispering, "Mariah."

I shake my head like I'm coming out of a sex induced daze. "What?"

"Your name. It's Mariah."

I look up into his heated dark eyes. The easy, arrogant smirk on his face makes me want to swat him, but I physically can't move. Instead, I lean forward and give into the urge of licking his chest. I giggle as I kiss it and pull away. I don't get far, though. He swats my ass on the way to the bathroom.

"Hey!" I shoot him what I hope is a sexy smile.

He winks and nods towards the bathroom door. "That shower sounds inviting."

My mouth drops. "Lyric is in there!"

He shrugs. "Not like you've never fucked around in the shower with her."

"I can neither confirm nor deny that."

He grins as he opens the door, disappearing inside. Moments later, I hear a squeal and a giggle, quickly followed by a low moan from Lyric and a deep groan from Matt. I bite my cheek as I head to the kitchen in search of anything to distract me from the images circulating in my mind. Images of Lyric's legs wrapped tightly around Matt as he pounds into her

87

while he holds her against the shower wall. Lyric's tits pressed against the wall and thrusting back against him as Matt pounds into her from behind. Lyric on her knees sucking him off...

I feel instant heat pooling in my lower stomach and between my legs. I'm tempted to join them in the shower, but the nagging voice that is responsibility niggles the back of my mind. I groan and rub my thighs together while my cappuccino finishes brewing. I look wistfully towards the bedroom, but the need to edit wins out. Judging from Lyric's and Matt's moans, I'm sure they'll be a while.

I've always been able to lose myself in writing. Whenever the outside world comes knocking, I throw myself into the alternate reality that is my characters. Their emotions become my own. Their lives are mine. I live and breathe my characters. It's what people say makes me a bestseller. Realistic stories. But, at least in my opinion, realism doesn't happen if a writer doesn't put themselves in the shoes of the characters.

I'm not sure how long I'm lost in my edit, but my reverie is interrupted when Lyric pounces on the couch and puts my laptop on the coffee table. She kisses me long and deeply, eliciting a moan from deep within my throat and a whimper when she pulls away. She bounce-walks out of the room. It's her fault both mine and Matt's eyes are focused directly on her tits, and that we watch her until she closes the front door behind her.

"She does that on purpose," I whimper. "She knows exactly what all of that..." I gesture towards the door like it's her glorious body. I bite my lip with a pout at not being able to finish what she started. "Does to people."

Matt laughs. "No. She doesn't. That's what makes her as sexy as she is." He leans down to kiss me. His hands teasingly trail up my thighs as his lips meet mine. His tongue dips into my mouth at the same time he grabs my pussy. I jerk against him as he squeezes my pussy and rubs while he smiles into my kiss. He kisses from my lips to my ear while he rubs. He squeezes once more. I quiver. His breath is hot against my ear. "Mine."

"Matt..." I grind against him, needing the relief, but he stops me, firmly holding me down with his other hand.

"I just made Lyric say it. Your turn. Say you're mine."

"Yours. I'm yours... Matt... please..."

He rubs his palm against my pussy with a chuckle. "I barely touched you," he teases.

I pant, gripping his shirt. "I'm so... I... you and Lyric... I'm so close already."

He kisses my neck. "Then you should probably come for me."

My thighs tremble as I bite his shoulder and come hard. I grip his wrist and squeeze my thighs around him as he squeezes and rubs his palm against me. "Matt..." My pussy clenches and pulses as I whimper quietly and moan.

He chuckles against my neck as I come down and release my vice like grip. "I can't let one of my girls come and deny the other what she so rightly deserves." He lets me go with a satisfied smirk as he stands.

"You might actually kill me one day with all of your..." I gesture wildly, unsure how to word what I want to say. "All of your... uniquely you."

He laughs again as he heads for the door. "Lyric is getting warmed up. Hurry up and clean up. I need you out there."

"Very well, Lieutenant." I give him a teasing smile as he comes back to pull me up. He swats my ass as I walk to the bedroom. I laugh.

A few minutes later, I walk out of the cabin. Matt has Lyric in some kind of a chokehold. I tilt my head and fold my arms over my chest as I watch.

"Like this?" Lyric puts her hand on Matt's forearm and pulls.

"No." Matt positions her hands the way he wants them, between her neck and his arm. "Like that. Now, do what I said." She pushes at his arm across her neck and gets nowhere. "See how no matter what you do, my grip is still strong?"

"Yeah." Lyric pouts and deflates. I can't help but smile at how adorable she is.

"Have you ever heard of 'sleight of hands'?"

She chews her lip. "You mean like in poker?"

"No. Not in poker. Not like a magic trick. It's when you're making your attacker think one thing, but you're really doing something else. Whenever anyone has you in a grip like this, they're going to think you're going to try and break free. Your natural reaction is to do what?"

"Get away?"

"How?"

"By getting your arms off me."

"But you already know you can't do that. I'm bigger than you. I'm stronger than you. So what are you going to do?"

Lyric huffs, frustrated. "I don't know!" She tries wiggling away and pushing his arms off her with all her strength. Matt only holds her more tightly, switching his position slightly so that one arm is around her waist and the other is over her neck. He holds her firmly against his chest until she stops fighting him.

I smile softly as I make my way towards them. I stop in front of Lyric. "Sleight of hands. You're trying to push his arm away from you, but you have a really nice height advantage. While your hands are occupied trying to push his arm away, stomp on his foot. Or you can back kick his knee. Or my personal favorite. Using one hand to punch him in the balls."

Matt lets her go and gestures to me. I take Lyric's place. He grabs me just as he had Lyric. "Don't fight me like you would in training. I'm not wearing padding. But I want you to show her."

"Okay."

"Go." Matt tightens his grip on me.

I put my hands up between my neck and his forearm, slowly so Lyric can see. Matt takes the hint and makes sure his movements are also slow. I fight against him for a few moments, wiggling and struggling like Lyric had. Matt's grip only tightens. I raise my foot and bring it down on his foot. Not hard enough to hurt him. Only to let him know my intention so that he can make his adjustment. His hand loosens on my neck enough for me to be able to slide my arms underneath his, giving myself the room between his arm and my neck I would need to breathe. I then use my foot to push back against his knee. Matt lets go and drops to his knees. I dart away and spin on him.

"I think I understand," Lyric says.

"Good girl. Now come here and try it."

Lyric does as he says, following my movements exactly. When Matt drops to his knees, I clap with pride and jump up and down like some high school cheerleader who just watched the quarterback score a running touchdown from sixty yards away. Lyric giddily smiles and rushes over to join me in my cheer. When this is all over, I may have to convince her to get her cheerleader uniform out and put on a show.

"Yes! I knew you could do it!" I hug her tightly as I bounce.

She hugs me back and excitedly turns to Matt. "When do I get to learn how to fight?"

"You never crawled as a baby, did you? You went from rolling around adorably on a blanket straight to running." He teases her, but I can tell he's just as proud as me at how quickly our girl is picking all of this up.

"We should teach her something. You never know. It might come in handy." I shrug as I look up at him.

"Okay. I'll teach you how to punch and kick without breaking your arm or leg. And maybe how to stun someone. Render them almost paralyzed for a few moments so that you can gain the upperhand and keep it."

"Okay!" she says, exhilarated as she bounces on the balls of her feet.

Matt starts teaching Lyric a series of kicks, making sure she's following through on each one and kicking as hard as she can. He shows her how to punch, making sure she's not punching with her hand, but with her entire arm. He shows her how to hit so that her knuckles and hand won't break. He, as with the kicks, makes sure that she's following through and using all of her body weight to her advantage in each strike.

He shows her where to aim her strikes. He tells her to aim her kicks to her attacker's legs and thighs; her punches to the chest and throat. The nose and groin. He makes sure she's holding nothing back when she strikes, though she's not striking him.

The longer we all practice the moves, the happier and more relaxed and confident Lyric feels. Her face lights up. Her eyes get brighter. I can tell she feels like the lessons will help her in defending not only herself, but me, and even Matt. I know her well. She hates the idea that she can't help us if we were to ever need it. She would feel like she failed if anything happened to us, and she didn't do her best to try and stop it.

"Okay. Let's talk about stuns," Matt says after we've all had a water break. He gestures to me. I walk towards him, resigning myself to the minor pain I'm about to feel for the next day or so. He gently grabs my waist and positions me in front of him with my back to his chest. He tilts my head to the left and runs his hand lightly over my neck. I shiver and smile softly. "See this area right here?"

"Yeah."

91

"That's your target. This area will stun her for a short time. It gives you the chance to gain the upperhand, especially if you don't have it, and keep it once you get it."

"Okay." Lyric's eyes are fixated on my neck.

"Stop thinking about licking it," I say with a giggle. "Just get it over with so I can take out my aggression on Matt for putting me through this."

Matt chuckles. "It's not that bad. Lyric, you're going to hit her with your forearm." He holds out his own forearm and shows her. "Fast. Hard. Don't worry about hurting her. She can take it. She's been through this before with a partner much bigger than you."

"Practice first, Lyric," I say softly, seeing her hesitation. "Just get the movement right. Matt can show you how."

"Sure." Matt moves behind Lyric and pulls her back into his chest. Lyric gives me a wicked grin and pushes back into his dick, grinding subtly. He steps back with a groan and swats her ass. "Focus."

She giggles. "Okay." He leads her through the movement a few times until she feels comfortable, then moves back behind me. I stand stock still, taking a deep breath and waiting for the hit. Lyric shifts nervously back and forth on her feet. "I don't want to hurt her."

"You won't, babe. Matt's right. I've been through it. My trainer was a little shorter than him and about his size. I can take the hit."

She moves into position but hesitates and then shakes her head. "I can't do it. I'm too afraid to hurt her. I'd never be able to hit as hard as you taught me."

I look up at Matt. "It might be better if she uses you as her target anyway. It's unlikely she's going to get into a fight with a tiny woman."

"You never know, baby. My hardest arrest was a woman who was under five feet. She was fast and feisty. Not easy to get a hold on. Sometimes, you never know where an attack is going to come from. But if you feel like you have less of a chance of hurting me than her, I'll take the hit."

"Good," Lyric breathes out relieved. "I feel better about that since I don't really know what I'm doing."

Matt switches positions with me and looks at Lyric. "Do what I said. Hit with your forearm right where I taught you. You got this." He looks back at me. "You gonna be able to catch me when I fall back? Or should I expect to be on the ground?"

I shake my head and smile at the charming, teasing grin he shoots me. "I got you."

"Good girl." He shakes out his body, eliciting a giggle from both me and Lyric. "Okay. Show me what you got, pretty girl."

"Okay…" Lyric steps forward and gets into position. I take a step back, positioning myself to catch the giant man in front of me. Lyric takes a deep breath, keeping her eyes on Matt, and strikes. Matt catches her wrist and pulls her into him kissing her. Lyric giggles as she melts against him.

I laugh. "Matt!" I swat his back playfully. "Take the hit. The sun is setting, and I'm starting to get cold with that breeze starting."

Matt pulls away as Lyric moans. "Okay. Okay. Let's get this done. At least you'll know how it feels to stun someone." We all get back into position. Lyric takes a deep breath and strikes Matt in his brachial plexus. Hard. Perfectly. Matt grunts and falls backwards. I catch him under his arms and move backwards with him until I'm on my knees in the dirt with his head in my lap.

Lyric straddles him with a giggle, and we both look down at him with bright smiles. Matt groans. "This will never happen again. Either of you tell any of the guys I work with that I got taken out by a girl, neither of you will be able to ride me for a year."

I burst out laughing as Lyric's mouth drops in mock surprise. "I thought you were going to say we won't be able to sit for a year." I lean down to kiss him. Lyric leans down to kiss him after me.

"Maybe I should get knocked out more often," Matt teases as he pulls away. I catch Lyric's hair and pull her back to me for a sweet kiss over Matt. "Especially if you guys make out over me."

Lyric and I giggle as we pull away from each other. Lyric teasingly grinds down against him before she moves off Matt as he groans and slowly sits up. I stay behind him in case he falls back again. We all slowly stand and brush ourselves off. Matt leads us to the porch and sits down between us on the swing. He swings it gently as he pulls us close to him, tucking us into his sides.

We watch as the sun sets over the water, the golden rays turning to brilliant shades of orange, red, and blue. Shades of purple and pink reflect off the water. The chill from the wind bites, but being tucked into Matt's side with his arm around me and Lyric's fingers entwined with mine, I've never been warmer. I've never been more calm.

For a little while, all of the world around us falls away, and if I let myself, I could believe that there are no dangers lurking in the shadows outside this perfect bubble we've created.

No one is after me.

No one can get to me.

Everything is perfect.

Chapter Eleven

✯ *Lyric* ✯

I never really thought I'd ever be happier than I was when Mariah and I decided to take our relationship further. Moving to the United States to be with her had changed my life so much for the better. I didn't think it was possible for my state of bliss to be lifted to a higher level because I never really believed I was missing anything.

Until Matt.

This. Right here. Mariah's fingers holding mine tightly resting in Matt's lap with Matt hugging the both of us to him as tightly as he is… Yeah. This is everything I've ever desired and so much more. I don't really know what I did to deserve a level of love that I've experienced with Mariah. I still don't know if I deserve it. But to be lucky enough to experience it twice? That's an entire other thing I sometimes don't feel worthy of. A love that I don't think I will ever be able to measure up to.

As the sky gets darker, it starts to get chilly. Mariah shivers as her phone goes off. She jumps slightly before reaching for it with a sigh. She lets go of my hand and sits up just as Matt's phone goes off.

He sighs as he picks it up. "I need to take this. It's DJ," Matt says.

He reluctantly lets me go as he stands. He leans down to kiss each of us softly before he walks into the cabin, answering his phone. I watch him go and move closer to Mariah, not ready to give up the physical contact I had so quickly. I cuddle into her side with a sigh, closing my eyes as I kiss her shoulder, and she scrolls to her messages.

"Oh my God…" I feel her tense.

Before I even open my eyes, I know instinctively that something isn't right. She tenses more and more the more she looks through the messages. The sounds she makes are strangled; getting quieter and quieter until she barely makes any noise at all. In fact, it seems to me that she's stopped breathing all together.

I can't figure out exactly what it is I'm looking at. There's picture after picture of a trashed apartment. Things are strewn everywhere. Glasses are broken. Plates are shattered. Couches are flipped. The TV is cracked on the ground. There are holes in the walls. In the bedroom, the bed is flipped over. The mattress is shredded. Clothes in the dresser are ripped and thrown messily around the room. The clothes in the closet are torn and hanging from the hangers in tattered shreds. The mirror in the bathroom is broken. Everything is on the floor. Windows are smashed. Everything is destroyed.

But that isn't all. As she is scrolling through the images, another message comes through. There are more pictures of another apartment with the same type of damage. Except it looks as if something may have been set on fire. I blink a few times until I finally realize who the apartment belongs to. My eyes widen and I shoot up, terrified.

"Oh my God! Matt!" I grab Mariah's phone from her hands. She squeaks and hiccups. I put my arms around her, hugging her tightly.

Matt pounds through the door as if he just found something out that we don't know yet. He has his gun drawn. His phone is to his ear. One eye is on us. The other is on the trees beyond the cabin. He sweeps the treeline with his gun as he positions himself in front of us.

"Get in the cabin. Stay behind me," he commands.

Mariah and I do what he says as he keeps his eyes out for any perceived threats. He keeps us both behind him, like he's some kind of human shield. As soon as we're in, he slams the door and locks it. He turns and pushes us quickly to the bedroom. He moves like a flash around the room, closing the windows and shades after he does a full sweep of the room, making sure there aren't any threats lurking in the shadows of the room.

"Stay in here. Don't come out. No one gets in here but me."

We both nod, shaking and unable to speak. We huddle near the bathroom, our arms locked securely around each other, both of us knowing that if anything comes in here, we might have a chance if we can somehow barricade ourselves in there. Our eyes are trained on the windows. Our ears are open for any movement we perceive isn't Matt.

I swallow, tightening my grip on Mariah. Whatever I was going to say has been long forgotten. Seeing him fly out of the cabin like that made the real reason we're here slam into me with the same amount of force as an atomic bomb. It takes my breath away. I unconsciously wrap my fingers in Mariah's hair and tug. She yelps. I jump, letting go of her hair. The phone I forgot I was holding dings with another message. I'm terrified to look, but something tells me I need to.

I gasp. My eyes widen at what I see. I drop the phone as if it's on fire. "No…" Mariah and I both jump and cry out, our eyes flying to the door as someone softly knocks.

"It's me, my girls. Let me in, please."

"Matt," I whisper. I gently tug Mariah with me to the door. Her eyes are wide and wild as I tug it open.

He ushers us both in as he holsters his gun and shuts the door behind us. I can do nothing but shakily point down to Mariah's phone on the floor as I lead her to the bed. She's just burst into tears. I want to, but I won't. I need to be strong for her. Matt leans down and picks up the phone. His expression grows somber as he scrolls through the pictures.

"Why is this happening?" Mariah asks miserably.

I'm pretty sure it's a rhetorical question so I don't answer. Matt sits next to us. He puts his arm around both of us, tugging us close to him. I don't realize how much I need his comforting touch until I feel it. I sink into Mariah, and Matt cuddles us close to him.

"That call I took was from DJ. He said they were called to the apartment complex on a noise complaint. Things shattering. People screaming. They thought it was a party. When they got there, the fire department was there, and there was smoke coming from one of the apartments on the upper floor. DJ was one of the first on the scene. He recognized the apartment as mine. After the fire department dealt with the fire, DJ went to check on the party call. He knew the apartment across from me is yours, so when he got there and saw the apartment number, he realized right away what happened. He called me right away."

"One of those pictures...," I whisper.

"It was my apartment. They torched a couch. Fire spread pretty quickly, but stayed in my apartment. Thank God."

Mariah sniffles. "I'm so sorry. This is all my fault."

"Mariah. Stop it," Matt commands. "This isn't your fault. It's none of ours."

Somehow the tone of his voice comforts me more. Gives me the strength to be strong, even though I want to fall apart. Mariah sinks into both of us with a heavy sigh.

I look up at Matt, gripping the waistband of Mariah's jean shorts. "They know." The words are so quiet, I barely hear them. I'm shaken by what I saw in those images. I'm terrified, but I hide it. I can't let Mariah see it. I won't let her see it. "About you. About me. They know who we all are now."

Mariah looks at me fearfully. "What?"

I don't take my eyes off Matt's. I can't. If I do, I'll break. I need him to be my anchor. "What do we do?"

"They don't know we're here. I've been pulled from the case, but DJ said he'd keep me informed."

"Why were you pulled?" Mariah asks. I can tell she's panicking, terrified like I am that we'll no longer have information coming in on what the gang is doing.

"Because you and Lyric and I are involved. They don't let officers investigate crimes against their family or spouses. Technically, that's what you're considered by departmental protocol. But DJ is keeping me informed. Okay? He's making sure I know everything they do. They know who we are, but they don't know where we are. None of us have the GPS on our phones turned on. We're off grid."

We all stay wrapped in each other's arms for God only knows how long soaking in each other's strength to get through it. Finally, Mariah moves. She stands slowly and stretches, looking longingly towards the bathroom.

"I really want to take a warm shower. Honestly, I think it would do us all good." She turns and gives us a watery smile. "Allow us time to think. Come up with a plan."

I chuckle softly, amazed at the strength of our girl. "Mariah's way of saying she'd like a little alone time to regroup."

She bites her lip as we both look up at her. "Sometimes, I just need it. I'm sorry…"

"For needing a little time to lose yourself? Please. We all need it. Go take your shower," Matt says softly, nodding to the bathroom. Mariah gives a weak smile and disappears behind the door. Neither of us say a word until she turns the water on. "What you saw in those images, baby. Just because they know who we are doesn't mean they know where we are. You need to know that."

The moment he's done speaking, I deflate completely and bite my trembling lip to keep myself from breaking down in tears. A few break through as I sniffle, unable to hold them back any longer.

Matt pulls me into his arms and hugs me so close that all I can concentrate on is him. His muscular chest. His strong arms. The way he's wrapped himself around me. The intoxicating scent of him mixed with all of the day's exertion that surrounds me. Fills me with a sense of comfort, and love. As if I could take on the world and still stand tall.

"You don't need to be strong all the time, baby. It's okay. It's okay to break down. I got you." He whispers the words in my ear. I wonder how he seems to know exactly how I'm feeling without me saying a word. He runs one of his hands up and down my back. The other holds me firmly to him.

"I… can't. I can't break. I have to stay strong. I need to be strong for her. She doesn't need to see how terrified I am. She needs to be able to lean on me. She needs me to be her strength."

"Ssh… You have me now. I got you. You don't need to be strong all the time. You're not doing this alone anymore. We can both be her strength. You can lean on each other and me. We're all together now. One cohesive unit. One family."

I crumble, burying my face in his neck and cry until I can't cry anymore. Matt holds me the entire time, rocking me back and forth, swaying as he whispers in my ear. I focus on his deep Southern voice. I focus on his cologne. On the scent that is uniquely him.

I slide one hand under his shirt and press my palm against his heart as I clutch his shirt in my other hand because I need it. I need that contact to center myself. I need to feel his steady heartbeat. To feel his steady breathing. To feel his strong arms around me. His soft but firm touch as he soothingly rubs my back. I need it to be able to calm down. To come back to myself. To be able to think. To focus.

After a while, I'm able to slow my breathing, to stop crying. I'm able to think clearer as I calm. As he calms me. His voice, his touch, his scent. They calm me quicker than anything I have felt before. I take deep breath after deep breath until I feel my heart steady. My grip on his shirt lessens, and I nuzzle his jaw as I relax completely, melting against him. I keep my palm pressed against his heart, almost grounding me as I focus back on him.

As the shower is turned off, Matt slowly pulls away from me. He runs his hand featherlight down my cheek. He looks at me with his intense dark eyes, and any unease that may have been niggling at me vanishes. I don't know how he does it. How he makes me feel everything with just one look. I feel comforted. I feel content. I feel loved. I feel safe.

"Feel a little better?" he asks softly as he tugs my hair gently.

I nod and smile softly, leaning up to nuzzle his cheek affectionately. "I do now. Thank you."

We both look up as Mariah steps out of the bathroom, a towel wrapped around her beautiful curves. I smile softly when I see how much she's relaxed since going in. It's like the tension melted away and washed down the drain.

"You're next, pretty girl," Matt says next to me as he delicately helps me up. I take Mariah's hand as I walk past her and give it a soothing squeeze. She gives me a grateful smile. I hate that the light in her eyes, in both of our eyes, is dimmed because of this situation. All because she was trying to do the right thing. Because of some buttheads. Buttheads who seem to forget picking on cops is a bad idea. It's unlikely the cop is going to lose the war even if he loses a battle.

I take a moment to relish in the hot water soothing my sore muscles as I step under the spray. I take a quick shower and make my way back to the bedroom. Mariah is tucked into bed, and I smile as Matt kisses me on his way to the shower for his turn. After I finish drying off and putting lotion on, I sit and start gently braiding my hair, keeping an eye on Mariah, peacefully sleeping.

Just as I'm about to crawl into bed, Matt's cell phone starts buzzing on the nightstand. I glance at it and realize I have no water next to the bed. I'm really rather thirsty. Hearing the shower shut off, I ignore Matt's phone, deciding he'll look at it when he comes out in a couple moments. I quickly make my way out of the bedroom, leaving the door open, just in case, to the kitchen where we have some bottles of water. As I'm grabbing one, I hear a loud crash, like glass shattering.

"Mariah?" I run into the bedroom. There's someone in all black clothing and a ski mask straddling her, pinning her to the bed, holding something over her nose and mouth. "Mariah!" I scream. I don't think. I don't hesitate. I run towards the person holding down my girl and smash the water bottle into his head as hard as I can.

"Ah!" he screams as he falls to the side, holding his head.

"Matt!" I scream. I struggle against the arms suddenly locked around my waist as I'm heaved off the ground and away from Mariah. "Matt!" Suddenly, I'm sailing through the air like a ragdoll and smashing into the wall. The wind is knocked out of me, and I gasp for breath, but I won't give up. I have to get to Mariah. I have to protect her. She's helpless!

I shake off the pain and scramble off the floor just as several other people jump through the window into the room. I kick and punch as hard as I can, just like Matt and Mariah showed me, but it's no use. There's too many of them. Just as I think I'm making progress, someone grabs me from behind and pulls me back, then pushes me away.

I elbow stomachs. I punch throats. I stomp on toes. I kick out knees. I punch more balls than I can count. I flail and headbutt. I bite. I claw. I scratch. I punch into chests and noses.

But I can't get to her. I can't get to my girl. I'm outnumbered and overpowered. I feel the towel I have on begin to slip off, but I adjust it quickly, refusing to let it fall, terrified what will happen if it does.

I see the fight in slow motion. Mariah's aura on the bed is like a bright light that's dimming by the second. I know I need to get to her before the halo of light around her is snuffed out. But I can't. Seeing her light dimming, I double my efforts to get to her. But no matter how much I fight, no matter how much I punch and kick and bite, I know instinctively it won't be enough.

Once again, I'm hauled away from behind. The person I knocked out on the bed is coming to. He looks at me. I can only see his eyes, but the pure evil emitting from them is unlike anything I've ever seen before. It's like it blazes into my very soul, freezing me in place. I can only watch from the floor I was once again thrown to as he leans down to her. I try to scramble back up. To stop him. But every time I do, I'm kicked back down.

From the corner of my eye, I see a black blur kicked across the floor in my direction. I turn slightly and silently gasp as I see Matt's phone. It must have been knocked on the floor and kicked around during the struggle. I slowly inch towards it, quickly grabbing it once it's within reach. I hide it underneath me as I blindly tap on the screen.

What seems to me like hours is really only seconds. All of the fighting I did took place so quickly, though it feels like it was so long. Matt comes slamming out of the bathroom with nothing but a towel around his waist at the same time the guy picks a drugged Mariah up and carries her out of the cabin.

In the distraction he causes, I glance discreetly at the screen and see I've managed to open the call log. I quickly tap on DJ's name, hoping to God that he picks up and hears what is happening. That he gets us help. I quickly clutch the phone to my chest, tucking it into the fold of the towel before any of these fuckers notice.

"Mariah!" Matt booms. He tries to get to her as I had. He fights off several guys before he's held back by four of them. He doesn't stop fighting. He throws them off only to be smashed in the head with a lamp by one of them. Matt drops like dead weight to the ground.

"Matt!" I scramble towards him, screaming. A pair of hands grab me, holding me back, and I fight to get free. I stomp on his foot and drop to the ground crawling towards Matt, terrified; knowing I have to fight.

I don't know who to try and get to. Matt or Mariah. I don't know if I should try and follow whoever grabbed Mariah, or if I should try to wake Matt. The hands grab me again, stronger this time, dragging me back.

Matt doesn't move. I don't know if he's dead or alive, but I trust Mariah is still alive. I believe they need her for something. I don't know what, but that belief makes the decision for me.

I have to get to Matt. He could be dying in front of me. I have to try and save him. "Matt!"

I fight and struggle to get away. To get free. To get to Matt. But it's to no avail. The grip whoever is holding me back has on me is too strong, and I'm weakened from all the fighting I've already been through. I'm starting to feel broken. Battered. My vision is starting to gray around the edges.

But I don't give up.

Matt is laying lifeless on the floor. Mariah is gone. I'm the only one who can get help for her. For him. I can only hope DJ has picked up the call and is sending help. I have to make it to Matt. I have to make sure he's okay, so I shake my head, clearing the blurring vision. I'm nearly to Matt when I feel something come down hard on the back of my head.

I whimper as I collapse, my hand just out of reach of Matt's arm. I pull myself forward as the gang is ordered to leave. I can feel the towel slipping off as they all make a hasty exit. I grab the phone from the folds of the towel I'm losing as I inch towards Matt.

I can barely hear it, but I think DJ is screaming, asking what's happening. "DJ... Help... Please...," I whisper, gripping onto Matt's forearm right before my whole world goes dark.

Chapter Twelve

☆ Matt ☆

I blink slowly and groan as I open my eyes. I slam them shut immediately when I feel bile coming up from deep within my stomach. The world spins. I grip whatever is under my fingers. Carpet? Fuck. I don't know.

Whatever it is steadies me, though, and that's all I fucking care about. It keeps me from falling off the fucking cliff I'm standing on. Or maybe laying on. Fuck. Maybe I'm hanging off of it.

It takes me a few minutes to come back to myself enough to be able to open my eyes. The pain in the back of my head is excruciating. It pulses and radiates in every direction, and I'm afraid to move too suddenly because I'm convinced my head won't follow the rest of me.

I blink again as I groan once more, taking in the chaos of the room I'm in. It's a complete mess. I remember the images of the destroyed apartment on Mariah's phone. For a few seconds, I feel like I'm there. In the middle of the disaster.

Mariah...

I put her to bed after we saw those images on her phone. She had just come out of the shower. Lyric had gone in. I rubbed Mariah's back and ran my fingers through her hair until she fell asleep. I went to the shower after Lyric came out. I took a quick one.

"Fuck…," I moan, closing my eyes through another stabbing pain, the intensity a level unlike anything I've ever come close to feeling. But I have to fight through it. I'm on the floor in intense pain with absolutely no recollection of how I got here. I don't know where Mariah or Lyric are. I have to get up.

Things are starting to come back to me slowly. I remember hearing a crash as I was coming out of the shower. There was commotion, and Lyric started screaming my name. I came bursting through the door barely remembering to wrap a towel around myself. I wasn't even dry. All I cared about was getting to my girls.

I came out when Mariah was being taken and Lyric was fighting like a damn warrior queen. I fought off the four guys holding me back and went for her, but someone must have knocked me out. The last thing I remember seeing was Lyric screaming my name and being held back by someone. She was terrified.

"Fuck… Lyric…" I force myself to move. Every cell in my body protests, but I need to figure out what happened to my girls. I start to push myself up.

That's when I feel it.

A soft hand on my arm.

I look at my arm and see Lyric laying on the ground. She looks like she's reaching for me. "Lyric!"

I feel the adrenaline coursing through my body. I push myself up and scramble towards her. As soon as I reach her, I see the blood coating her hair. I see the bruises on her body from where she was thrown. The scratches from the fight.

"Matt!" I jump nearly out of my skin when I hear the front door slam open and hard footsteps pounding across the floor. "Matt, where are you?!"

"DJ?" I don't dare hope I have back-up arriving this quickly. I haven't called anyone. But I swear that's his voice. He runs into the bedroom like a fucking knight; the gun in his hand like a gleaming sword. He looks down at me after he sweeps the room. "Fuck, am I glad to see you."

DJ looks behind him and holds up a hand. "Stop. Clear out here." He takes off his black, leather jacket and hurries into the room to cover Lyric. It's only then I realize she's completely naked. The towel she had on is underneath her. It looks like it slipped off as she was crawling towards me. Clutched in her hand is my phone with an open line to DJ.

"They took her," I say as I continue checking Lyric. I'm happy as fuck she's breathing, but she needs to be taken to a hospital.

"I know. I tried to warn you. I called about ten times. No one answered your phone. I called Mariah's. I called Lyric's. I thought I was too fucking late."

"Please tell me you brought paramedics."

"No. But we can lay her down in the back of the squad. I know it's cramped, but if you get in there and put your legs across the seat, leaning against the door, you can cradle her back there with you. Get something on and get something for her. I'll take her out."

I do what he says because if I don't, I'll lose my fucking mind. It's racing in a thousand different directions. I know Lyric will be okay. The head wound doesn't look that deep. But I don't know where they fucking took Mariah.

After I grab a bag with a change of clothes for Lyric, I sprint out to the car. I don't acknowledge any of the other officers who are combing the property for any clues they can find. I can't allow myself to. I have to force myself to trust they'll find Mariah so I can take care of Lyric.

I crawl into the back of the squad with Lyric, situating her between my legs as I lean against the door. DJ jumps in the driver's seat and takes off, racing for the hospital. I keep Lyric wrapped in my arms.

"Where did they take her, DJ?" I ask.

"We found their hideout. We think they took her there. I have Brody and Link there."

I look at him, a little surprised. "You? Since when does Brody let you lead investigations?"

"Since I told him I'm taking this one since he pulled you off. He didn't like it, so I went to the Chief. Fuck him. He's a great guy, but he was trying to cut me out because he knows I tell you everything. Chief gave me the case because he said he'd want someone doing that for him if he were in your position. Made me promise to keep your ass from doing something stupid, but gave it to me anyway."

"I'm grateful, DJ. You don't know how much. I'm doing everything I can to keep my attention in this squad, and on Lyric."

"I don't blame you, but you can trust me. She saved my life, Matt. I'll die saving her if I have to."

"I know." I say the words quietly as I nuzzle Lyric. I kiss her ear and hair. "Fuck, baby, please wake up. I can't get through this without you."

⭐⭐⭐

I run my fingers soothingly through Lyric's hair and glare at the clock on the wall. Two in the morning. All we know is where Mariah is. They confirmed they arrived at the warehouse, but they couldn't get to her without her getting hurt. They keep telling DJ they have to plan out the best way to get in.

Meanwhile, my girl is having God only knows what happening to her. The fucker who carried her out didn't bother making sure she had clothes on. She was naked. Completely fucking naked. Her towel was still on the bed. I saw it when I was getting Lyric's clothes after I changed.

Thinking of what they could be doing with her right now has every cell in my body on edge. My blood is boiling through my veins, but with every second that passes, I can feel it turning more to ice than fire. The only thing keeping me from flying completely out of control is Lyric laying in my lap.

She woke up in the squad on the way to the hospital saying Mariah's name and crying. My heart shattered. I wasn't able to hold back. I held her close to me with my face buried in her hair and cried with her the entire way to the hospital.

She nearly had a panic attack when she was getting checked out by the doctor. I almost forgot how much my girl hates hospitals and doctors. She wouldn't go anywhere without both me and DJ flanking her. Even when she was brought to a room. At first, the thought of DJ seeing her naked while she was being examined sent all of my possessive genes directly to the surface. It wasn't until after she told me why she wanted him there that I allowed it.

107

It was because of me. She wanted both of us to be checked out, but she didn't want either of us to be unprotected when I was having my injuries dealt with. She didn't want me out of her sight, and she didn't want DJ out of the room just in case we were attacked. I couldn't deny her the sense of security he brought.

Neither of us wanted to stay at the hospital. After being cleared by the doctor, we left. We couldn't go back to the apartment, so DJ brought us to his house. Lyric felt dirty from the fight and being at the hospital. After we both cleaned up, DJ gave her a t-shirt to wear. When I grabbed clothes before we left the cabin, I wasn't thinking clearly. I only grabbed a pair of jeans and a bra for her. She didn't want to sleep in either of them, so she's just wearing the t-shirt.

I look up at DJ, unaware of half the things he had just said. All I can think of is I don't know where we'd be if he hadn't picked up. If he hadn't acted as quickly as he had, I don't know that we'd know where Mariah is.

"You haven't heard anything I've said, have you?" DJ asks.

"No. I haven't, man. I'm sorry. My mind is on Mariah. Now that I know Lyric is okay, all I can think about is getting our girl back. I keep thinking about what they're doing to her. I... Fuck."

"I get it, Matt. But you can't think of that. You have to concentrate on getting her back. Come on. Help me. You lead so many entries with SWAT. Tell me how to get in."

I look down at the images he has on the table. He's not wrong. I'm one of the commanders with our SWAT, and there's a reason for that. It's because I'm so fucking good at it. I can spot weak points and come up with ways to enter any building or house.

It's almost like my mind scans the blueprints, and I become the building. I can see every angle. Every corner. Every hidden crevice. I live and breathe the structure.

I scan through the blueprints, not moving from my place on the couch. Not pausing in my methodical stroking and light tugging of Lyric's hair. I'd never admit it, but my fingers running through her hair are just as much to calm me as it is her.

Like a beacon, the weak spot pops out at me. Almost like it's being highlighted on the page. I carefully lean forward, mindful of Lyric, in order to get a closer look, and to check and make sure I didn't miss anything.

Sure of what I've found, I nod. "There." I point to the truck entrance of the warehouse.

DJ shakes his head. "Heavily guarded. Already looked."

"No. I'm talking about the window by the backdoor. Here." I use a marker to circle the window. "Measurements have it about five feet off the ground, but it's large enough to fit through. And it's around the corner from the truck entrance."

DJ looks at it hesitantly. "Are you sure?"

"Definitely. Look. Here's the truck entrance. Here's the door people can go in and out of. This is what they would have heavily guarded. But if you look here," I pull out another picture of the surrounding area. "There are trees that brush up against this whole side. It's about thirty feet from the truck entrance and ten feet from the door. It's hidden completely by the trees. I doubt Brody or anyone he has with him would see this because they spend so much time looking at the surveillance images over the blueprints."

"And they wouldn't see this in surveillance because of the trees hiding it."

"Exactly. You want an in? There's your point."

"I'll take it to Brody. You gonna be okay?"

"Bring my girl back, DJ. I'm having a fuck of a time not storming the place myself. The only thing holding me back is Lyric. I can't leave her alone. I won't. I'm trusting you to bring Mariah home, DJ. I..." I take a deep, shaky breath. "I don't know what I'll do if I lose her."

DJ stands. "You won't. We won't. I won't let it happen. You know how much I care about her. About you. About Lyric. You know I'll do whatever it takes to bring her home." He squeezes my shoulder and reaches down to run his fingers through her hair as he grabs all of the images and blueprints.

He grabs his extra gun and heads out the door. He pauses in the doorway and gives me a look full of determination and something else I can't quite put my finger on. I watch him, instinctively knowing that not only can I trust him, but that he'll do whatever needs to be done to save her. Besides Lyric, that's the only thing that gives me comfort.

A few minutes after DJ leaves, Lyric shifts and slowly wakes up. I look down at her as she whimpers and sits up. She plasters herself to my side and sniffles. I can do nothing but hug her as tightly as I can. I can't comfort her with words because I don't want to lie to her. If she asks if Mariah will be okay, I won't know what to say.

"Is she home yet?" Lyric whispers.

"No. I wish I could say yes, but they haven't gone into the building. They're trying to find a way in without hurting her. They know where she is in the warehouse, but other than that, nothing has changed."

She's so quiet for a moment, I have to look down to make sure she's still with me. Finally, she looks up at me, teary-eyed. "I was so scared, Matt."

"I know, honey."

She grips the waistband of my sweats like they're her lifeline and shakes her head. "No. I mean, yes. When they came in, and they took her... I was scared. Terrified. But I fought. I felt like I failed her for a little while, but I know now that I didn't. I fought. I got us help. I knew I had you to help get her back. That's what got me through. But... when I saw you... laying... there... I thought you... were..." She bursts into a fresh bout of tears and buries her face in my chest.

"Hey. Hey, honey. I'm right here." I pull her into my lap. She straddles me and buries her face in my neck. I hold her so tightly, I'm not sure she can breathe. She holds me just as firmly. Neither of us let go.

"I wouldn't... have been able... to know what... to do..." She sobs so hard into my neck that my shirt is soaked in seconds, but I don't give a fuck.

"Baby, I'm right here. I'm okay. You're okay. We're going to get our girl back." We have to because if we don't, I'm not sure either of us will survive it. But I won't tell her that.

"I couldn't have -"

"Shh... Baby. No more talking. No more thinking. I'm right here. I'm safe. You're safe. And we're going to get Mariah back if it's the last thing I ever do. I promise."

"I thought you were dead. I thought I was alone. I couldn't lose you, too." Her entire body trembles, and she tightens her grip.

"I'm not. I'm right here. You can feel me, baby. I'm here."

Lyric crushes her lips to mine, tangling her fingers in my hair. I keep my arms firmly around her so she's pressed as tightly and closely to my body as I can make her be. She kisses me long and hard. I let her, sensing she needs it to make sure I'm still alive. She grinds against me and kisses me harder. Deeper. I respond to her instantly, unable to control it; unwilling to do anything about it.

Lyric reaches down and grabs my dick. I moan, but any words I planned to say are cut off when she crushes her lips to mine again, barely giving either of us time to catch our breaths from the last kiss.

She tugs my sweats down, freeing my dick. She gives me no time to react before she slams down on me, taking my entire dick into her soft, warm, wet as fuck, tight pussy. She doesn't pause after she takes my length inside her. She spreads her legs slightly and thrusts her pussy hard and fast over my dick at a furious pace.

"Fuck! Lyric! Jesus…"

I fumble a little to grip her hips, attempting to gain some semblance of control over her erratic movements, but it's a useless maneuver. The way she clenches and pulses. Her moans. Her soft sighs that turn to screams of pleasure and ecstasy.

Instead of slowing her down, I thrust harder and deeper into her. My nails dig into her hips, and I slam her down onto my dick in time with each and every one of my thrusts.

"Matt! Yes!"

She twists her hips, spreading her legs as wide as she can, taking me deeper than I've ever been, and slams down on top of me as I pound her pussy. I tug her hair. She tugs mine. She clenches around my dick. We both scream out. I slap her ass hard.

The sex gets wilder. The dominant side of me screams to take back that control, but I can't. I couldn't stop it if I wanted to. She feels too good bouncing on top of me. Her pussy tightening and pulsing around me gives me everything I need but didn't know I needed in this moment.

She has no idea what she's doing, but every slam of her pussy onto my dick, every thrust I give her, gives me more and more strength to get us both through this. Every clench. Every pulse. Every scream. Every scratch of her nails down my back. My arms. My shoulders. Every slap of her ass. It all fills me with the energy I had sapped from me. The toughness I need to keep Lyric and I from falling apart.

Her thighs start to shake as she digs her nails into my back. Her pussy clenches so hard that moving my dick from deep within her is impossible. I bury myself inside her and nip her neck as she trembles and shakes. I look back up at her. She looks at me pleadingly as she moves herself furiously back and forth over my dick with the sexiest moans and whimpers.

"Come for me, beautiful," I say, burying my face in her hair.

"Matt!" she screams. She comes so hard, she rips my orgasm from me. My dick thickens and throbs in time to every clench and pulse of her pussy.

"Fuck, Lyric!"

I slow the thrusts down as we both shiver and tremble. We pant as we catch our breath. I kiss her neck as she moans and hums into my shoulder. Her nails in my shoulders lessen as my own, dug into her hips, retract. Our hips jerk against each other as we slowly start coming down.

"I… don't know what came over me. I'm sorry," she whispers, her breath hot against my neck.

"Don't apologize for needing to be close to me after an experience like that, baby. I needed it just as much as you did."

"Is it wrong that I feel better now? Stronger?"

"No. Because so do I."

I lock my arms around her waist again. She wraps hers around my shoulders. We both bury our faces in each other's necks. I don't pull out, sensing she still needs to feel me like this. She still needs the connection. Needs to make sure I'm still real and breathing.

Truthfully, if I were to admit it, I need it just as much. Half of me feels like it's missing. I know Lyric feels the same way. Not being able to be a part of getting our girl back kills me. If I didn't have the distraction of Lyric, if I didn't need to be here to take care of her, I wouldn't care what anyone said. I'd be out there bringing home our girl.

"They better not have hurt one hair on her beautiful head," Lyric growls, mimicking my own thoughts.

"If they did, they'll answer to me."

"I'll rip their balls off and make them swallow them before shoving their pathetic excuse for dicks down their throats to choke on."

I chuckle, but I don't doubt the truth behind those words for a second. "And I'll tear each and every one of them apart. One at a time. Limb by fucking limb."

I don't need to look at her to see there's a dangerous fire in her eyes that mimics my own.

When it comes to Mariah, there's no limit to the lengths either of us will go to bring her home.

It's the same we'd do for each other.

Chapter Thirteen

☆ Mariah ☆

I open my eyes slowly, nearly overcome with dizziness and nausea. I shiver against the cement floor. I've woken up a few times since I was thrown in here, but I've been in and out of consciousness. I don't have a clue where I am. The room is so dark I can't even see my hand in front of my face.

I managed to find a wall in a corner that I think is as far away from the door as I can get. There's a very faint strip of light coming through what I've decided has to be the door to the room. I hug my knees to my chest with my back against the wall, making myself as small as possible.

I can feel how dirty and grimy the wall and floor in this room are because I'm completely naked. I know I was taken by the gang that's been after me, but I don't understand why they haven't tried to do anything to me yet. It makes no sense to me why the one I assume is the leader keeps telling everyone to stay away from me.

I'm grateful. Whatever the end game is scares me, but for now, I'm more than thankful that he's keeping everyone away from me. I'd fight to the death if anyone did try to come near me, but I know I wouldn't be able to fight them all off.

I hiccup as my heart races out of control once more. It's been happening off and on ever since I was thrown in this room. I've forced myself to fight through it, even though my heart feels like it's going to beat so fast it won't be able to keep up with itself and stop all together.

I take another breath of the dank air and nearly throw up. The smell of grease; the faint smell of gasoline overwhelms my senses, but I fight. I have to. I refuse to give up. I refuse to believe I won't make it out of this alive. No matter what I have to go through. I've been through far too much shit in my life to let it end this way.

I shiver against the cold again, but I keep forcing the deep breaths. I keep my body as tightly curled up as possible and breathe in the warm air I'm exhaling against my skin. I focus on Lyric's body wrapped around mine. Matt's strong arms holding us both close to him.

Protectively.

Possessively.

I've never felt I belonged to anyone but myself. The idea that anyone had any type of control over me had always been so viciously nauseating to me. It wasn't until Lyric came into my life that I wanted that feeling of belonging to someone. Of loving someone so incredibly much that the idea of being apart was unthinkable.

I didn't expect to feel like that once in my life. The fact that I feel it twice, with both Lyric and Matt, is something I never believed would happen. Sometimes it's staggering. Especially when I feel the intensity of the love I have for them reflected back on me every second of the day.

Thoughts of Matt and Lyric manage to calm me down once more. Instead of passing out into a state of blissful dreams, though, my body rebels against me. The exhaustion doesn't overtake me. Suddenly, all of my attention is on how cold I am. The uncontrollable shivering and trembling overtake my being. I try thinking nothing but warm thoughts.

It doesn't work.

The thought of hypothermia setting in scares me so badly. I've never been near this level of fear, and it sends me into another panic attack. I can fight off the gang members. I can't fight off hypothermia. It's an invisible enemy that I won't be able to attack once I feel its claws.

I will my body to stop shivering and trembling. I will my stomach to stop clenching and shaking. I try to keep the tears from falling again, but it's pointless. They fall anyway. If I had the energy to wipe them away, I would. But I don't dare give up the little body heat I have left. Letting go of my knees and uncurling in any manner will probably send my body into shock. I've fought through so much already, but I'm not sure I can fight that.

I look up when I hear voices and footsteps. They're faint... So faint. But I can tell they're getting closer and closer. I steel myself for whatever I'm about to face this time when they come through that door. I make my heart cooperate because I have no choice. I won't give them the satisfaction of seeing me fall apart. I won't let them see any vulnerability. I won't beg them to let me go. I won't let them see me cry.

What they don't know is I have two secret weapons on my side. I have Lyric and Matt. I know they won't give up on me. I know they'll search the ends of the Earth for me. They'll leave no stone unturned. No crevice unsearched. I know they're doing whatever they can to help me. Until then, I have to do whatever I can to survive.

For them.

For me.

So, I watch the door. I listen. I listen for any movement. I listen for how many footsteps. I listen for voices. It sounds like two people this time, but there's something different. Something... off. This time it sounds like... something is dragging. Like... I perk my ears up and close my eyes as I listen. I can't quite make out the voices, but I know they're dragging something with them.

"I still don't understand what the fuck your deal is with this bitch. She's the reason Slick's in jail and didn't pass his last initiation test. Yet you're protecting her for some reason."

The voices are close enough to make out now. It sounds like the one I've decided has to be second in command. He's the only one who seems to get away with talking to the leader like a friend instead of a God or something.

"Still acting like a newbie. Fine. You want to know? The girl is the girlfriend of a cop. We can use her for leverage. Get Slick out by buying off the investigating cops. Only we won't be paying them. We'll be assuring her safety. Even trade. We get him. They get her. Cops do whatever they can for each other and their families." The leader's voice makes me sick to my stomach. He has a slight accent I can't place. I haven't seen him long enough in the light to be able to figure out his ethnicity, but I know he's definitely not all caucasian.

"Oh... Yeah, that's good."

"I know. That's why I'm the leader, and you aren't."

"What about the other chick? Why didn't we take her? She could've been fun for us."

I can hear him sigh exasperated as they stop outside the door. I brace myself and put my head back in my arms. I'm hoping if I make it look like I'm still passed out, they'll go away. That whatever reason they're here has nothing to do with me. I'm sure it's far-fetched, but I can dream.

"You're fucking stupid. Do you know that? I don't know why I put up with you. Because she has nothing to do with this. Because taking her would have caused more problems for us. She fucking bites."

"So? I like them when they fight."

"Fucking imbecile. Taking her would've made the cop go ballistic. I thought she was a roommate, but I think he's fucking both of them."

"Lucky asshole," the other guy grumbles.

"We didn't take her because while she may have been of some use, she would've fought the whole way. We didn't have time for that. You know how close we were to getting caught. They all started pulling in within minutes of us leaving. If we'd taken her, she would've gotten us caught. All of us. I still don't understand how they got there so fast. Now stop asking questions. Get this fucker in there."

"What are we going to do with him?"

"I don't know. He's pretty fucking stupid to just walk in here like that. But he's not the priority. We'll deal with him later."

I furrow my brows in confusion but keep my head down as they open the door. Seconds later, I hear something sliding across the floor.

"What a waste. Fuck, we could have fun with her." He sounds so sad. The bile rises in my throat. I swallow it down and hold perfectly still. They close the door.

I hear them walking away. Their voices become more and more distant, but I don't dare move until I can't hear them anymore. I wait until there's absolute silence before I take even a single breath. I raise my head and look around. It's not easy to make out anything, but I'm hoping that if

I let my eyes adjust and concentrate hard enough, I'll be able to see whatever they threw in here.

My mind takes off with a thousand different possibilities. A bomb? Some kind of gas to knock me out? A snake? I freeze and let out a terrified gasp when I hear what sounds like rustling or... slithering?

"Oh, God..."

No... Wait, Mariah. Calm down.

I can practically hear Lyric's and Matt's voices in my head. They said *he*. *He* walked in. Whoever he is, it's not an animal going to kill me. At least not the actual animal kind. It could be the human type of animal. Maybe one of their enemies. Maybe a rival gang.

No. They wouldn't put someone in here who might kill me. They said they needed me for leverage. He won't let his own gang members touch me. That has to count for something. It has to. I have to believe it does. It's the only thing forcing me to focus.

"Mariah? Where are you?"

I... I'm dreaming. That... no. It can't be. I shake my head. I have to wake up. I can't survive if I'm sleeping. I squeeze my eyes shut and pinch myself. Hard.

"Ow..." I rub the sting away.

"Mariah? Are you hurt? Talk to me. I can't see you. It's too dark. You need to talk to me."

It can't be... It can't. "D... J?" My teeth chatter with the sudden intense wave of emotion.

Relief.

It washes over me like a waterfall. Or maybe that's the cold. Maybe my body temperature has dropped so far that I'm delusional. I'm shaking so viciously now.

"Mariah. Come on. Where are you? I've got an idea of where you might be. Talk to me so I can follow your voice."

I don't know if I'm in a dream or reality, but I force myself to speak. "Here... in the... corner."

"That's it. Keep talking, honey."

My teeth chatter as I sniffle and hug myself. "I'm so c-c-cold. So cold."

"I know. I'm here." I feel a hand on my leg. I jump a little before I see him. The outline of a dark angel.

"Oh… God… DJ…" I break down in tears as I grip his solid frame.

"You're fucking freezing. I don't know why, but some fucking small part of me thought maybe they'd be decent enough to give you a blanket, or even a sheet." I feel him moving next to me, though I can't totally tell what he's doing. Moments later, I feel him tugging something over my head.

"DJ? What are you doing?" I'm starting to question myself. Maybe it's not DJ. Maybe I did dream it. Maybe they're tying me up and are going to take me somewhere. I choke on a sob and cough.

"Hey… Honey, ssh… I'm just putting my shirt on you. It's warm. You need to warm up."

I stop struggling and nearly deflate as he helps me into the long sleeve shirt. He helps me stand up and brushes the dirt off me. It's then I realize he literally gave me the shirt off his back. He sits against the wall and tugs me down into his lap, so my butt isn't touching the floor. He wraps his arms around me and puts his leather jacket around me like a blanket. I feel myself immediately start to warm.

"DJ, you can't. You need to stay warm. It's so cold."

He pulls me closer to him and surrounds me with himself. "Good thing I have you to keep me warm then. Body heat. We'll both benefit from it."

DJ sits with me, wrapped around me, unyielding. Not only do I start to warm up, but I start to calm down. I can feel myself fall into a deep, deep trust in him that I've only ever felt with Lyric and Matt. I've never allowed anyone fully into my circle of trust until them. But DJ… He just walked into the dragon's den to save me. I've been hesitantly getting to know him, trusting him slightly more and more as the days go on. But no more hesitation. From here on out, I know I can trust him fully.

"How did you get in here?" I ask after a while.

"I got Matt to show me what our team wasn't seeing. We needed a point of entry. I brought it to Brody. He hesitated. I told him that he needs to trust that Matt knows what he's talking about. He sent someone to investigate. I told him that I'm not waiting any longer. They needed a distraction. So, I gave it to them. I walked in. Got myself caught. I knew they wouldn't touch me. At least not much. I knew I'd take a few kicks and punches, but I played like I passed out. I knew they'd take me to you."

119

"DJ…" I can feel the tears again, but I reach up and wipe them away as I shake my head and speak quietly. "You sacrificed yourself. You didn't know what they would do to you."

"Call it a cop's instinct. All I knew was that you saved my life that night. I wasn't about to let you go through this alone. I saw an opening. I took it."

"It was reckless. They could've killed you."

"It was a risk. A calculated one. I'm trusting my team. And you need to trust them, too."

I'm quiet for a moment, feeling safe and protected now that he's here. I warm more and more, unsure how long we sit here. My head snaps up when I hear several footsteps running down the hall.

"Check the rooms! All of them!"

"Here comes the calvary," DJ whispers in my ear as he tightens his grip.

My stomach drops with a whoosh. Like I just went down the longest and farthest decline on a rollercoaster ride before coming to a complete, lurching stop. I look up as the door crashes open, but I don't jump. Instinctively, I know it's DJ's team. I watch as they sweep the room with high-powered rifles with scopes and lights. I sink into DJ.

"Clear!" one of them yells. They all stand guard as Brody strolls into the room. He shoots a glare at DJ, but underneath is obvious relief.

He points a finger at DJ and growls, "You're fired."

"I'll take it. She's safe."

"What the fuck kind of stunt was that?" Brody booms.

"You needed a fire lit underneath you. I saw my in." DJ gently nudges me forward so he can stand. He carefully helps me to my feet as Brody comes over to us. He wraps us both in a bear hug.

"Fuck, do you know how worried I was?" he asks. He tightens his grip. "About both of you."

"Judging by the fact that neither of us can breathe? I think we get it." DJ chuckles as Brody releases us.

"Fuck. I'm recommending you for an award." Brody says.

DJ laughs. "Forget you fired me, old man?"

"Fuck you. Let's get out of here. Let's get Mariah home. Before Matt kicks my ass, and Lyric burns down the city." Brody turns to lead us out of the room.

"Just the city?" I ask, smiling softly. "If I know Lyric, she's already burned down half the world trying to get to me. I'm pretty sure Matt has cleared a path for her."

DJ and Brody laugh. DJ wraps his arm around me as I hand him his jacket. He pushes it back and shakes his head as someone hands him a shirt. He puts it on. I curl into his jacket when he helps me into his car, buckling me in.

"Ready to go home? Well, my house. For now."

I nod, tears of joy filling my eyes. "I just want my loves."

He smiles and kisses my forehead. He closes the door, jumps in the driver's side, and takes off for his house.

To the missing pieces of me.

To my loves.

To my heart.

Epilogue

☆ *Lyric* ☆

(One Year Later)

I run my fingers through Mariah's hair as I look down at her. I can't get over how beautiful she is. How a year after she was kidnapped, she's only managed to get stronger. More gorgeous. Sweeter. Everything she already was magnified to some unnatural level reserved only for her.

"You're staring again," Mariah says, a soft smile tugging at the corner of her mouth.

"I was thinking."

"Of ravishing me?" I know she's joking, but she doesn't know how close to the truth that is. I always want to ravish her. If she knew how often, I'm sure she'd think I'm crazy.

"No. Not really. Well, sort of. More... how much you've accomplished. Even after what happened."

Mariah turns onto her back and sits up. She kisses me long and deeply with a soft moan. Her tongue slides into my mouth and starts a familiar dance that always leaves me breathless and needy. I suck softly on her tongue as my most intimate parts light on fire. She pulls away. I whimper and look at her with heated eyes.

She runs her thumb across my bottom lip and smiles. "Beyond being kidnapped, nothing happened. And they've all been arrested. They're all going away for a very long time. The leader was killed in prison in some kind of gang rivalry thing. His second was killed when he was hit by the car running away when SWAT showed up. I won't stop living life because some asshat tried to mess with it." She kisses me again, just as the door to our new house opens.

"I'm home!" Matt calls from downstairs.

"Up here!" I yell excitedly.

"Besides," Mariah says, tugging me down onto the bed. She scrambles between my legs and thrusts her tongue inside my pussy hard. I jerk my hips and grab her hair. "I don't think either of you would let me wallow in self-pity."

I can't respond. All I can do is tug her hair and arch into her as she thrusts her tongue into me over and over again until I'm writhing underneath her. I've hardly noticed Matt has come into the room.

Through my hooded eyes, and my lust-filled haze, I barely make out Mariah's scream as he enters her from behind, but the vibration goes straight through my core and sends me hurtling to the edge. I hold back, though. I want to enjoy every second of every lick, nip, suck, thrust, and hum.

I grip the sheets as I look down at Mariah. By the wickedly delicious smile on her lips as she buries her tongue in me again and again, I'd say she's enjoying every second of making me come undone.

"Come, honey…," Matt pants. He reaches over Mariah and flicks my clit.

"Oh! Yes… Matt!" Mariah screams against my pussy as she comes.

It's all I need to give her what she wants. "Mariah!" I arch off the bed and come hard for her. My pussy clenches and pulses around her tongue as she moans and hums. I tug her hair a little harder and scream.

I don't really have a chance to finish my orgasm before Matt has shifted. Matt thrusts hard into me. I moan when I feel his cock fill me. Mariah is straddling me with her hands gripping our headboard. She looks down at me as she lowers her pussy to my mouth. I waste no time diving in. I love how she tastes.

"Oh! Lyric…" She grinds on my tongue as I grip her hips and move her at the same furious pace Matt is pounding into my pussy.

"Oh… fuck! Matt!" I wrap my legs around his waist, meeting his hard thrusts. I purposefully clench around his thick dick and relish in every jerk and moan it brings from him.

"Shit… Lyric." Matt's eyes are rolled to the back of his head as he shifts his hips back and forth and slams into me harder and deeper. Faster. Just the way I like it.

Mariah reaches down and pulls me up into her pussy. I nip it and slap her ass. "Lyric! I'm… gonna… Oh!"

I can feel her clenching uncontrollably as her pussy pulses and her thighs shake. I'm right there with her. The purposeful clenches of my pussy has turned into a raging inferno of pulses. I feel Matt's dick thicken to an impossible size, filling me unlike anything I've ever felt. He grips my hips and lifts me higher as he thrusts even harder into me.

"Fuck… Come with me, my sexy girls," Matt grunts as he buries himself in me. He pulls Mariah to him and kisses her long and hard. I feel him come hard as I start clenching and pulsing coming just as hard as him.

"Ah! Matt!" I scream. I grip Mariah's hips, digging my nails in her ass as she screams into his kiss and comes around my tongue.

We all fall against each other panting and wrapped up in each other as we come down.

✮ ✮ ✮

Hours later, as the sun is setting over Gainesville, Mariah, Matt, and I are all sitting on the balcony off our bedroom. I've spread a blanket out for us with a small spread of crackers and cheese. Sparkling champagne is chilling in a bucket. We're curled next to Matt with his arms wrapped around the both of us. Mine and Mariah's hands are entwined and resting in Matt's lap.

"Can you believe it's been a year already? Since the three of us ended up in this relationship?" Matt asks as he leans in to kiss both of us on the forehead. "Sometimes I still can't believe it's real."

124

"Me either," Mariah says quietly, cuddling into his side and squeezing my hand. "Everything was perfect with just me and Lyric. I can't believe it got even more perfect with you." Mariah lifts our hands to her lips and kisses my palm.

"I still don't really know what I did to deserve either of you. I don't understand how I got so lucky," I whisper, smiling softly as I nuzzle Matt's chest and bring Mariah's palm to my lips, planting a soft kiss onto it

"I'm not sure how I got so lucky either, or if I truly deserve this type of love," Matt says as he shifts. He reaches for the bottle of champagne and pops the cork. It flows over the side of the bottle, and Lyric and I both giggle. Matt smiles as he pours us each a glass, keeping them in front of him. He puts the bottle back and hands us each a glass as he sits back.

I lean my head on Matt's shoulder. "A toast?"

"More like… a promise." Matt looks down at his glass. Mariah and I look at each other slightly confused. "A promise that I'll love and protect you. For all my days. A promise that no matter what life throws at any of us, I'll never stop honoring you. I'll love you more each day. Until my last breath."

He lifts his drink to his lips with an almost imperceptible smirk. Mariah and I both hesitantly lift our glasses to our lips as we watch him. A glint of something in his glass catches my eye. I gasp, my eyes widening. I look into my own glass and Mariah's and see it. Tears spring to my eyes.

"Matt…," I whisper.

"Hmm?"

Mariah sees what I did as she sips the champagne. "Matt!"

Inside mine and Mariah's glasses are matching diamond rings set on a platinum band. The diamond shines brilliantly as it catches the light. Matt fishes his out of his glass as Mariah and I both excitedly pick ours out. I put it onto my left finger without waiting another moment and hold it up, admiring it. It's then I notice that Matt's matches ours. Each of ours is set with small blue diamonds that match the blue strip in Matt's ring.

Mariah and I both jump on Matt without restraint. We kiss him all over his face and neck until he laughs and physically pulls us off him far enough so that we can look at him. He leans in and kisses each of us in turn.

Deeply.

125

Passionately.

All of the love we all feel for each other, and all of the love and desire and passion he feels for us, is spilling from our lips into the kiss. When he pulls back, we are each left breathless.

We don't need any more words. There aren't any strong enough to express what any of us feel in that moment anyway.

As I cuddle into Matt, Mariah's hand finds mine once more. I'm completely baffled about what I did to deserve either Mariah or Matt. I'll never understand what I did to end up so blissfully happy with two of the most amazing people in the world. I don't know how I'll ever be worthy of either of them.

But I know without a shadow of doubt, I'll spend the rest of our lives proving myself deserving of it.

The End

Next In The Beautiful Dream Series

The sweet and sinfully sexy Beautiful Dream Series continues with
Softening Lyric

I'm a Lieutenant with Gainesville Police Department and a Commander
with our SWAT team. My job is my life, and I like it that way. No chance
my heart can get broken.

As fate would have it, my Captain drops Lyric Sharpe into my lap. Her
Field Training Officer is out with an injury, so guess who gets stuck with
her?

Me.

She's a sassy new recruit. A brat who doesn't take orders and challenges
me on every level. I hate it because it appeals to every part of me that
needs to be in control.

Before I know what she's done to me, Lyric has burrowed into the cockles
of my cold heart. I want to spend all of my time with her.

In typical Matt Chance fashion, though, I make a mistake that shatters all
the progress we've made, causing her to flee right back into the fog she had
just managed to escape from.

I refuse to give up on her or us. Hopefully, I can make it to her in time
before I lose her forever to the clutches of the demons who haunt her.

Order ***Softening Lyric*** Today!

The Beautiful Dream Series

Available Now

Loving You
My Love, My Heart
Softening Lyric
Undercover Temptations
Captain Charming
Breaking Boundaries
Crashing Into You
Tactical Inferno
Ravishing Our Queen
Cherished By The Texan
Unveiling Our Passions

Box Sets Available

The Beautiful Dream Series: Box Set: Part 1
The Beautiful Dream Series: Box Set: Part 2

Other Books By Melony Ann
The Crane Family Series

Available Now

The Reluctant Mafia King
Sweet Lies
Billion Dollar Love Story
Be Mine
Protecting Her
Dangerously Forbidden Love
His Heart
Love In The Dark

Box Sets Available

The Crane Family Series

The Deimos Trilogy

Available Now

Connor's Legacy
Aryan's Alpha
Kade's Redemption

Box Sets Available

The Deimos Trilogy

The Forbidden Temptation Series

Available Now

The Detective's Forbidden Temptation
The Running Back's Forbidden Temptation

The Lucinio Family Series

Available Now

Rising From The Ashes
The Player's Rebel
Encrypting My Heart
Fighting My Fate

Multi Author Series
Piper Falls: Firehouse 49

Available Now

Ignite My Fire by Melony Ann
Regain My Fire by Kindra White
Playing With My Fire by D.L. Howe
Fight My Fire by Darley Collins
Against My Fire by Anneke Boshoff
Relight My Fire by Louise Murchie
Harness My Fire by Ayana Lisbet
Quench My Fire by Havana Wilder

Let's Be Friends

Follow me on

Bookbub

Facebook

Goodreads

Instagram

Tik Tok

Visit my website
www.melonyannauthor.com

Subscribe to my newsletter and get a FREE never-seen-before NOVELLA
just for subscribers!
https://www.melonyannauthor.com/exclusive-content

Join my Facebook Reader Group!
Melony Ann's Sizzling Book Nook
https://www.facebook.com/groups/melonyannssizzlingbooknook

The official Beautiful Dream Series Playlist on YouTube
https://youtube.com/playlist?list=PLGEiD5wbQmDe1z4_FeeKbMLcBkOz
1M4L4

Dedication

Trust and love is what we seek. We find all of our desires in your eyes.

Acknowledgements

Brad - Every single book I try to come up with words to express how I feel about you. And every time I come up lost. And then I realized that's it. Without you, I'd be lost. Because without you, I'm not sure I'd have had the courage to express my feelings for her. My heart will always be yours. I love you.

Laura - I often spend the last few moments before bed trying to figure out how I deserve the level of love you show me throughout the day. Like you, I'll never believe that I'm worthy of you. But I promise to try every day to be worthy of the love you have and the love you show for me. Because without you, there isn't a me. I truly and whole-heartedly love you. I'm yours.

Jay - Whether you're near or far, I always feel like you're right next to me. You've always been here for me, and I'm not completely sure I'd be functioning as well as I am on most days without the feelings you manage to invoke in me each and every single moment of the day. As it does with Laura and Brad, my heart belongs to you. I love you.

Anneke – I love being able to fall into your books and lose myself for a while. Thank you for being that for me.

Jason - The world may crash, but we're always holding each other up. Love you.

Kayla - I'm so honored to have you in my life cheering me on. Love you.

To the Bookstagram Community.

To my family.

To all of those who believe in me and support me.

137

To all of those who don't.

Cover by: Carter Cover Designs

Edited by: Alyssa Skaggs

About Melony Ann

Melony Ann began writing short stories and poetry as a child. She continued honing her craft over the years until she took the plunge and began publishing her work, despite having severe anxiety.

Melony writes contemporary romance stories that are full of suspense and a lot of steam.

When she isn't writing, she is loving her family and working to make her life something she deserves.

Melony believes that if her writing can inspire just one person, then all of her hard work is worth it.

Her hope is that her writing allows each and every one of her readers to escape for a little while. To dive into a different world one book at a time.